NIHARIKA

A STRANGE STORY OF LOVE & RESPECT

ADITYA MISHRA

Contents

Acknowledgements   *xi*

Prologue   *xiii*

1. Emty Field   1

2. Dear Diary   28

3. Inebriation   47

4. First Date   69

5. Birthday   100

6. Encounter   119

7. I Love You   145

8. Respect   165

Epilogue   179

Lord Shiva has a plan for you, so be happy and enjoy your life.

Har har mahadev..

"Utha kar dekh deewar apney jhutey mahal ki

Dafan mera ashiyan milega tujhey, chuur, ae
maghrur."

Aditya Mishra

To all the survivors of narcissistic abuse,

This book is dedicated to your strength, resilience, and courage. May you find healing, hope, and the power to reclaim your life. Your journey is a testimony to the human spirit's ability to overcome even the darkest of times.

With deepest respect and admiration,

Aditya Mishra

Acknowledgements

Writing this book has been a journey filled with challenges and triumphs, and it would not have been possible without the support and encouragement of many wonderful people.

First and foremost, I would like to thank my family. To my parents, Santosh Mishra and Rajesh Mishra your unwavering support and patience have been my rock. Your belief in me kept me going even when I doubted myself.

I am also grateful to my friend, Aditya Sengar for his constant encouragement and for being my sounding boards. Your honest opinions and late-night brainstorming sessions were invaluable. I would like to thank Tushar Sharma from the bottom of my heart who understood the vision of this story and designed the cover page

Lastly, I would like to thank my readers. Your enthusiasm and feedback have been a driving force behind this book. I hope you find as much knowledge and joy in reading it as I did in writing it.

Thank you all for being a part of this journey.

Prologue

These were the days when the clouds appeared to be in a playful and romantic mood. Occasionally, it would begin to drizzle, tiny droplets gently kissing the earth, creating a sweet melody of drip-drip. This drizzle would often escalate into torrential rain, suddenly pouring heavily. It felt as if the clouds and the rain were engaged in a playful dance, teasing and chasing each other like a newlywed couple, brimming with joy and mischief. It seemed as though the earth had spread its arms to convey the emotions of the drops falling from the sky.

The entire scene was a stunning interplay of nature's elements, with clouds, rain, and earth all joining in this grand display of affection and emotion. It was a moment when the world slowed down; everyone paused, no vehicles on the road, no birds in the sky, all to appreciate the simple yet profound beauty of this exquisite scene and the rain.

Some people found this game spiritual, while others began to fear it, and some even criticized this season. We are all made of clay; we breathe the same way, we eat the same way, and we do everything that a human being should do. Still, a question troubles the mind: why does every person's thinking differ? What would happen if everyone's thoughts were not different? Whatever occurs, whether good or bad, perhaps you will find the answer at the end of this story.

I decided in my childhood that I would become a psychologist and help those who truly need it. After passing the CUET exam, I went to stay at my aunt's house in Ajmer for a few days. My aunt's daughter, who had shared so much with me since childhood, was now getting married. Although she was three years older than me, she had always been my best friend, and we used to share everything with each other.

I used to spend most of my holidays in Ajmer with my cousin Sarika. Growing up in Delhi, I often visited my aunt's house in Ajmer to escape the noisy life of the city. My aunt was a teacher, and my uncle worked as a government employee. Sarika was very intelligent in her studies; she was the kind of girl who always excelled in everything. However, Sarika Didi had a kind heart and never boasted about her good marks.

I am sharing so much about Sarika because she was the first guide in my life who inspired me to become a psychologist, a story I will share another time! Today, this journey also began at her house, which changed my life forever.

Today marked three days since I arrived in Ajmer and restlessness plagued my mind, troubling me and fostering an unknown nervousness that gave rise to strange delusions in my heart. This time, I felt a strange emotion in my heart. I don't know why, but instead of heartbeats, it felt as if a drum was playing within me. It seemed like something significant was about to happen, and I felt trapped in a storm with no way out.

Sarika Di and I had gone to the parlor today and also did some shopping for her wedding, so we were quite tired. As soon as we reached home, we went straight to her room.

"What happened to you, Niharika? I've noticed that ever since you arrived in Ajmer, you seem a bit restless. Is everything alright in Delhi?" Sarika di asked me while combing her hair.

"I'm not sure, Di," I started uncertainly.

"There's a heaviness in my heart that I can't shake off. It's unlike anything I've felt before. Initially, I thought it might be something physical, like acidity, but it's not that. It's something different, something deeper." After saying this, we both laughed out loud, and I closed my eyes and lay down on the bed.

Sarika di leaped onto me and exclaimed, "Boyfriend?"

"Nah, it's nothing like that, but seriously, there's something I can't understand." Saying this, I got up and went straight to the balcony, standing there.

Following me, Sarika Di also came to the balcony and stood beside me. Today, it was lightly raining, and the park in front of Sarika Di's house looked very beautiful.

"Come on, let's go to the park," I urged.

"First, eat something; we will leave after dinner. I am feeling hungry," Sarika said, holding my hand as we both went down and sat at the dining table where everyone was already seated.

"Aunty, what have you made? Who eats ridge gourd?" I exclaimed as soon as I opened the casserole.

"So what do you want to eat, pizza, a burger, and what do you call that strange dish that keeps smoking?" A beautiful girl entered through the door and finished my aunt's sentence by saying, "Sizzler".

"Ah!! My true daughter is here!" Aunty exclaimed as she hugged her and guided her to sit beside me.

She held a plate of sizzler in her hand, and since I felt like a rat was jumping in my stomach, my full attention was on her plate of sizzler. Even if my life depended on it, I was not going to eat Ridge gourd and miss the chance to enjoy sizzler.

"How are you? And how's your father? Did that doctor's medicine make any difference for him?" When aunt asked the girl, she felt a bit sad.

But she replied respectfully, "I am fine, but I no longer believe any doctor can cure my father. Only a miracle can set things right now."

Sarika Di interrupted her and said, "Divyasha! Never lose hope; it's the only mantra I've learned since childhood. Being older than you, I'd like to suggest the same."

I tried to see and understand something, but the aroma of the sizzler plate the girl had brought was preventing me from thinking about anything else. At that moment, I was unaware that this plate of sizzlers would soon smoke up my life and trigger an earthquake I had never even imagined.

"Excuse me, but have you brought this plate of sizzler for us?" I interjected, capturing everyone's attention.

I realized I had made a mistake, but I had complete faith in Sarika di's ability to handle the situation. I looked at her with wide eyes, knowing she would come through as she always does.

"Divyasha! I am sorry we forgot to introduce you to my cousin Niharika! She lives in Delhi and is going to be a psychologist soon." Sarika Di introduced me to that sweet girl, Divyasha.

"Hi! Niharika di, yes, I brought this for you all." Divyasha said this and put that sizzler plate on the table, saying, "Please have it."

Without wasting a single second, I started eating the sizzlers, and it was awesome. "Divyasha, this is amazing. You are a master chef." I said this and again started eating.

By the way, let me clarify one thing: I am not a girl who eats a lot; it's just that I have been starving since afternoon. So finally we had our dinner, and then, as per the promise, Sarika di asked me to visit the park, but I was so tired that I preferred to sleep.

"Good night, di. I am going to sleep," I said to Sarika di.

"Good night!" Sarika di replied while talking with her fiancé over the phone call with a flying kiss.

"Is this for me or Jiju?" As usual, I teased her.

"Obviously, for you, he doesn't believe it; he wants more." Saying this, Sarika Di turned her back, and I went to sleep.

The next morning I took my cup of coffee and stood on the balcony to enjoy the pleasant weather. When the light drops of rain fell on my face, it felt as if someone had brought me amidst the clouds.

While I was enjoying my coffee and the rain, my eyes fell on a man walking in the park, and that man was walking while smoking a cigarette. At first, I laughed after seeing him, and then I started feeling a strange agitation in my heart as if I had a years-old relationship with that unknown man.

My smile suddenly turned into sadness, I was not feeling good seeing this. So when I turned to go inside, I saw Divyasha on the balcony of a nearby house. I called her by gesturing with my hand but she was also staring at that man so she didn't look at me.

I called out to her, "Hey Sizzler Girl!"

She turned to me and asked, "How are you, Didi?"

"I'm good, Divyasha. How about you?" I responded.

"I'm fine, Didi," she said with a smile.

Then she picked up the cup from the table and headed inside.

"Okay, Didi, I have some work to do. Please come to my house in the evening with Sarika Didi. I'll cook something nice for you to eat, and we can talk about Delhi. I miss my friends there," she said.

Then, looking at the man walking alone in the park in the light rain, she added, "Please come, Didi. I'm leaving now."

She raised her hand to say goodbye to me, but I pointed towards the man and said, "What a strange man he is. Actually, I would say he's not just strange but crazy." With that, I started laughing loudly.

"Yes, he is crazy," she said with a slight smile before walking away.

I went inside and lay down next to Sarika Di, trying to wake her up. However, she had been up late last night, so my efforts were in vain. Unable to sleep and with no one to talk to, I decided to go to Divyasha's house to pass the time. I picked up the plate of sizzlers she had brought over last night and headed to her place.

As I rang the doorbell at her house, my heart pounded like the Shatabdi Express. It felt like something significant was about to happen, but I couldn't figure out what. I calmed myself and kept ringing the bell. When Divyasha didn't answer after the second ring, I turned away in disappointment. Just then, I saw the same man from the park standing behind me, completely soaked and holding a cigarette in his mouth. His physical appearance reflects his inner qualities: he is charming, elegant, and his features seem as if they were sculpted by angels. I stood there, staring at him.

"Who do you want to meet?" he asked, crushing his cigarette in a large flower pot by the door.

Controlling my racing heart, I said, "Divyasha."

I had never imagined that the man who seemed crazy from a distance would be so handsome up close. My heart beat even faster, and I couldn't understand this feeling. I wasn't scared of him at all; instead, I felt like telling him to take care of himself, avoid roaming around in the rain, and cut down on smoking since it's harmful to health. But I just stood there, mesmerized.

He moved towards me, bent slightly, and opened the gate. As he did, he said, "Come inside, I will call Divyasha. Please, have a seat." With that, he went inside the room.

The room was cozy and inviting. Soft, warm lighting filled the space, casting a gentle glow on the wooden furniture. A plush sofa sat against one wall, adorned with colourful cushions. There were a few framed pictures on the walls, adding a personal touch. A large window let in the sound of the rain outside, creating a soothing ambiance. The air smelled faintly of fresh flowers, likely from the vase on the coffee table. It was a place that felt both comfortable and welcoming.

After about two minutes, Divyasha came out. By then, I had carefully examined the pictures in the drawing room and realized that the man was her father. I felt foolish for thinking he was crazy. Feeling embarrassed the first thing I did when Divyasha appeared was to say,

"Sorry," without any hesitation.

Divyasha reacted with a sweet smile and reassured me, saying, "It doesn't matter, Di. You haven't said anything wrong. I've heard a lot about Papa from people." Her kind response made me feel a bit more at ease despite my initial embarrassment.

"I just came to return these utensils," I said, handing them to her. "I'll come back with Sarika Di in the evening." Then, feeling guilty, I left without looking back.

I had returned home, but I couldn't stop thinking about that man's face. Perhaps it's because I'm a medical student with a passion for psychology. I kept finding different excuses to think about him. I told myself that maybe I was just curious about his story or that I wanted to understand his behavior better. I even thought that perhaps I was just trying to distract myself from getting bore. Ultimately, my mind settled on the fact that I'm 23 years old, and seeing a handsome man can certainly stir my hormones.

I went to take a bath while Sarika Di was still sleeping. Even as I stood under the shower, I couldn't stop seeing that man's face in my mind. I quickly finished my shower and went to wake up Sarika Di.

"Wake up, you've been sleeping for so long," I said, grabbing her and shaking her gently but firmly.

Sarika Di slowly opened her eyes and, still half-asleep, asked, "Has there been an earthquake or something?" Her groggy response made me chuckle a bit, despite my urgency.

After her initial groggy question, Sarika Di rubbed her eyes and sat up. She looked at me with a mix of curiosity and concern and asked, "Why are you in such a hurry? Did something happen?" Her tone was more alert now, sensing that I had something important to share.

"Yes, wake up now, you've slept too much," I said, waking up Sarika Di.

"What happened? Why are you so upset?" Sarika Di asked.

"Nothing special, I just feel something strange," I replied.

"Okay, tell me one thing, who lives in the house of the girl who came yesterday?" I asked.

"She is Geeta Aunty's granddaughter, Divyasha. She came here to live with her father a few months ago," she replied.

"What happened to her father?" I asked.

"It's a very long story, but I'll tell you in short," she replied.

"He is Geeta Aunty's son. Years ago, he had a love marriage and moved to Delhi. But his wife made his life miserable. She wouldn't let him work and slowly started controlling him. Before marriage, he was a confident young man, but after a few years, he began to experience strange feelings and changes. Uncle stopped talking and started blaming himself for everything. A once cheerful and lively person has now become a living corpse. His wife lives alone in Delhi, while Divyasha moved to Ajmer with her father. She is consulting a good psychologist, but there hasn't been any significant improvement yet." She said.

"Oh my God, that's so heart breaking. I can't believe how much they've been through. Poor Divyasha having to handle so much at such a young age. It's so unfair. I really hope the psychologist can help her father eventually. It's just so sad to see someone lose their spirit like that. Thank you for telling me, Sarika Di. I feel so bad for thinking he was crazy. I'll definitely be more understanding from now on." I replied.

When I asked further, Di explained, "Her father just keeps thinking, walking, and smoking cigarettes. Poor Divyasha, only 20 years old, has to take care of her elderly grandmother and troubled father. Despite this, I've never seen her sad; she always keeps smiling. Mummy tells me that her father was the same way—always happy and laughing. The daughter is just like her father."

Hearing this, I felt a deep sense of empathy and concern for Divyasha and her family.

I said "That's so heart breaking, Di. I can't imagine how difficult it must be for Divyasha to handle all of this at such a young age. It's incredible that she manages to keep smiling through it all. It must be so hard for her, especially seeing her father like that. I really hope things get better for them soon. Thank you for sharing this with me."

Sarika Di almost started crying as she said this. She wiped her tears and added, "Now let's go shopping; only a few days are left until my wedding." She pulled my cheeks, touched my forehead lovingly, and went to the washroom."

"Di, what is his name?" I asked Sarika Di while standing at the washroom door.

"Bhaskar," she said from inside.

Usually, hearing someone's name doesn't affect me, but for some reason, Bhaskar's name echoed in my ears. It felt as if someone had called out his name from the top of a high mound in an empty desert, and its echo sent a shiver through my entire body.

Later that evening, after returning from shopping, we went to visit Divyasha at her home.

"This is for you, Divyasha," I said, handing her a gift I had bought while shopping. Ever since Sarika Di told me her story, Divyasha had been on my mind. The gift was a painting of a girl alone in a forest, surrounded by tall trees, walking forward all by herself.

For almost half an hour, we engaged in normal conversation, but my mind kept drifting back to the mystery of what had happened to her father. How had such a handsome man become so silent? After some time, Sarika Di's phone rang. She made an excuse, went to the corner of the room, and started talking. Now, it was just Divyasha and me sitting in the living room.

Seeing an opportunity, I asked, "Is this your father in this picture?"

She picked up the frame from the table and replied, "Yes, my father, my love, my life, and everything."

"Don't mind me asking, but there's no picture of your mother. Is she okay?" I asked, pretending not to know anything about her.

"Yes, she is fine. She lives in Malviya Nagar, Delhi," she replied politely and calmly.

"I'm going to be a psychologist soon. I just took my CUET exams last week," I said, hoping she might share something about her father. But she didn't. Perhaps she had lost hope that her father would ever laugh and talk like he used to.

I had just started talking when Sarika Di came over and asked me to come back home with her because she wanted to talk to Jiju. I refused and, holding Divyasha's hand, asked her, "Can I stay here with you for a while? She's going to talk to Jiju for more than an hour, and I'll get bored. If you don't mind, I'd like to stay with you."

"Yes, why not," she replied, holding my hand. We both said goodbye to Sarika Di and sat back down on the couch.

Before she could ask me anything, her father came out, gave a small smile to Divyasha, opened the gate, and went out.

"I'm sorry about the other day; I didn't know he was your father," I said, apologetically.

"You are not the first one to say that. Although you said it unknowingly, people often deliberately tell me that my father is mad," she said, bowing her head.

"Please don't be sad. I didn't mean to upset you. I said it unknowingly, but now I want to know more about him. As I mentioned, I'm soon going to be a psychologist, and I would be very happy if I can be of any help to you," I said, hugging her.

I was almost in tears. I don't know why, but I could feel her pain. I've never felt like this before. It's a very strange feeling, as if I'm alone on a ship in the middle of the ocean, with the cold wind making my body tremble.

I felt such deep empathy for her situation because of the immense burden she carries at such a young age. Hearing about her father's drastic change from a confident, happy man to someone who is now silent and troubled was heartbreaking. The fact that she has to take care of both her elderly grandmother and her father, while still managing to keep a smile on her face, is incredibly touching. It made me realize how strong and resilient she is, yet also how unfair her circumstances are. This combination of admiration for her strength and sorrow for her plight stirred a profound sense of empathy within me.

After a moment, we embraced each other, and she led me to her room. Divyasha took out some photographs from her cupboard, showing her father as a happy person.

I was stunned to see these pictures because the man I met was nervous, sad, and lacked any enthusiasm. His old photos radiated freedom, spontaneity, and confidence.

"He wasn't always like this. He was a very happy and joyful person, but due to my mother's cruelty, he became the person everyone now calls crazy," she said, starting to cry.

Seeing those old photographs filled me with a mix of emotions. I felt a deep sadness for the man who had lost his joy and confidence due to such harsh circumstances. It was heartbreaking to see the stark contrast between the vibrant, happy person in the photos and the troubled man I had met. At the same time, I felt a strong sense of empathy for Divyasha, understanding more clearly the pain and loss she must be experiencing. It made me even more determined to support her in any way I could.

As we looked through the photographs, Divyasha shared some fond memories of her father's happier times. She talked about how he used to take her to the park every weekend, where they would play games and have picnics. She also mentioned how he loved to sing and dance around the house, filling their home with laughter and music. These stories painted a picture of a loving and joyful man, making the contrast with his current state even more poignant. It was clear that these memories were very precious to her, and sharing them brought a mix of smiles and tears.

I consoled her and asked, "What did your mother do?"

"Her narcissistic tendencies led him to this condition," she replied, starting to gather her father's pictures.

"I'm so sorry you're going through this. It sounds incredibly tough." I said.

My mind was filled with images of his once-smiling past and his current, withered state. I hugged Divyasha, I said "If you need someone to talk to or just be with, I'm here."

Then left and returned to my aunt's house. I couldn't sleep the entire night and spent hours reading about narcissistic disorder and abuse on the internet. I wondered whether this could actually be a form of human being.

Actually, narcissistic individuals can seem monstrous because they often make life miserable for those connected to them. They don't believe in helping but rather in destroying the lives of those they control. Long-term abuse can lead to anxiety, self-doubt, and other mental health issues. Narcissistic abuse often causes emotional trauma, deeply affecting a victim's mental health over time. Like other forms of psychological and emotional abuse, it can lead to anxiety, depression, and post-traumatic stress disorder (PTSD).

It's like a big house that looks strong from the outside, but what happens if its walls become hollow inside? What if there are cracks in those walls? If rainwater seeps through or if the roof collapses, it would be terrifying. Imagine being inside that house with no option to escape during an emergency. You just sit and wait for the walls to collapse. This situation can produce numerous negative thoughts in the human brain. The same goes for a person living with and experiencing abuse from someone with narcissistic personality disorder (NPD).

CHAPTER ONE

Emty Field

Today, I woke up with a heavy heart. The first thing that came to my mind was Bhaskar ji. It was only 10 o'clock, but I felt an urgent need to talk to someone who could help me understand what I was feeling. I decided to call my coaching teacher, who used to take psychology classes. I thought he might be able to provide some insights.

"Hello, Jai Sir. Can you tell me something about narcissistic behavior?" I asked him directly, skipping any pleasantries or inquiries about his well-being.

"Niharika, it's 10 a.m. I was just about to leave for the institute. I'll call you back once I get there," he replied before disconnecting the call.

I went to the balcony and stood there, noticing that Bhaskar was roaming in the park. I quickly ran down to the kitchen where aunty had already prepared tea. I picked up a cup and quietly made my way out to the park in front, hoping that today I would finally get a chance to talk to Bhaskar and understand why he has changed so much.

The sun dipped below the horizon, casting a warm, golden glow over the fields. The leaves rustled in the gentle breeze, and distant laughter echoed through the park. I sat on the bench, my hands trembling slightly as I watched Bhaskar. He stopped, took out a cigarette, and lit it, the flame briefly illuminating his face. The aroma of freshly brewed tea lingered in the air, mingling with the scent of blooming jasmine. I took a deep breath, trying to steady my nerves. "I need to talk to him," I thought, my heart pounding in my chest. I didn't want to miss this opportunity. Since I had come and sat on the bench, he had passed in front of me three times.

"Excuse me, can you give me a cigarette?" I mustered up the courage to ask, my voice trembling slightly.

Yes, I smoke cigarettes sometimes, so I thought this might be a good way to start a conversation. However, this approach also failed. Bhaskar lit a cigarette, the flame briefly illuminating his face in the dim light. He gave me a small, enigmatic smile, one that spoke volumes without uttering a single word. His eyes, though silent, seemed to carry a weight of unspoken emotions. Then, without a word, he started walking away, leaving a trail of smoke behind him.

I sat on the bench, my eyes following him, trying to decipher the meaning behind that smile. The park around me was alive with the sounds of rustling leaves and distant chatter, but all I could focus on was Bhaskar. After about 15 minutes, my phone rang, breaking my trance. It was Jai Sir. I quickly picked up the call, hoping for some answers.

"Yes, now tell me what you wanted to ask. I was late today, so I couldn't talk," he said, his voice slightly breathless from the rush.

"What can you tell me about narcissistic behavior?" I asked, my voice tinged with hope and curiosity.

"A mental health problem called narcissistic personality disorder (NPD) affects how you relate to people and how you see yourself," he began, his tone serious and informative. "An overwhelming urge to feel important or impress others is characteristic of NPD. That urge may be strong enough to encourage dangerous actions that harm both you and everyone around you." He paused for a moment, and then added with a note of caution, "Such people are very dangerous; I suggest you keep a distance from them if you have someone like that in your life."

"Okay, sir, but these days I've met a man whose wife is a narcissist. He seems completely normal in appearance, but I can't read his psychology. Please help me," I asked, my voice filled with concern and curiosity.

"Abuse by narcissists can take many different forms," Jai Sir began, his tone serious and measured. "It can range from verbal and financial abuse to emotional and psychological abuse. A victim of any of these types of abuse may experience significant and enduring effects on their mental, emotional, and physical health. These are signs of either narcissistic abuse syndrome or narcissistic victim syndrome."

I interrupted him, eager to understand more. "What are some of the specific signs and effects of this kind of abuse?" I asked, hoping for a clearer picture.

"Victims often suffer from anxiety, depression, and a pervasive sense of self-doubt," Jai Sir explained. "They might experience flashbacks, intrusive thoughts, and hypervigilance. The constant manipulation and control can lead to a deep-seated fear of upsetting the abuser, resulting in chronic stress and even physical symptoms like headaches or insomnia."

He paused, allowing the weight of his words to sink in. "Narcissistic disorder is very dangerous,"

"Bhaskar is my aunt's neighbor. He just keeps walking and smoking cigarettes. He doesn't talk to anyone much, but if someone talks to him, he smiles," I explained, recounting everything I had observed about Bhaskar so far. His solitary walks and the constant presence of a cigarette between his fingers painted a picture of a man lost in his own world.

"It's hard to tell without talking to him how he'll be able to recover. But I can explain some general symptoms that might help you understand more about him," Jai Sir replied, his voice thoughtful.

Without wasting a minute, I said, "Yes, sir, please. I want to know more about him."

"I can't tell you more about him specifically, but I can share some general symptoms," he continued, his tone shifting slightly as if he sensed something unusual in my behavior.

"Ohh!! Yes, sir, actually I want to know more about this disorder," I said, trying to cover up my emotions.

"People with narcissistic tendencies often exhibit a range of behaviors," he began. "They might have an exaggerated sense of self-importance, a deep need for excessive attention and admiration, and a lack of empathy for others. They often monopolize conversations, belittle or look down on people they perceive as inferior, and expect special treatment. Behind this facade of confidence, they are usually very fragile and sensitive to criticism."

As he spoke, I could almost see Bhaskar's silent, enigmatic smile in my mind, and I wondered how much of what Jai Sir described applied to him. The park around me seemed to fade away as I focused on every word, hoping to find some clue that would help me understand Bhaskar better.

"How can I find out?" I asked.

"Okay, so the first thing to understand is that a person's self-esteem can be severely and subtly impacted by narcissistic abuse," he began, his voice steady and informative. "A narcissistic person's relentless assault of criticism, belittling, and manipulation can progressively erode the victim's sense of self-worth. As the abuse continues, the victim might begin to believe the harsh things the narcissist says, making them feel inadequate and defective. Over time, a victim may start to mistrust their own abilities and fear making mistakes, which limits their personal and professional development."

"Okay, so that might be why he doesn't talk much," I said, trying to piece together Bhaskar's behavior. "And?" I prompted, eager to learn more.

He continued, "Emotional trauma brought on by narcissistic abuse frequently has a long-term negative impact on the victim's mental health. Similar to other types of emotional and psychological abuse, it can result in post-traumatic stress disorder (PTSD), anxiety, and depression. These mental health problems may also cause victims to have difficulty controlling their emotions, leading to mood swings, angry outbursts, or emotional numbness."

As he spoke, I could almost see the layers of Bhaskar's silent suffering unfold before me. His solitary walks, the constant smoking, and the rare, enigmatic smiles all started to make sense. The park around me seemed to blur as I focused on Jai Sir's words, hoping to find some way to help Bhaskar.

"Victims often feel trapped in their situation," Jai Sir continued, "and the constant manipulation can make them doubt their own reality. This can lead to a state of learned helplessness, where they feel powerless to change their circumstances."

I nodded, even though he couldn't see me. "That explains a lot," I murmured, more to myself than to him. "Thank you, sir. This really helps."

"Remember, Niharika," he said gently, "understanding is the first step. But professional help is crucial for recovery. Encourage him to seek therapy if possible."

"I will, sir. Thank you so much," I replied, feeling a mix of relief and determination.

In my mind, I was thinking about Bhaskar—why he smokes so much and why he walks endlessly. The questions swirled in my head as I tried to make sense of his behavior.

Jai Sir continued, "Because of the well-studied mind-body link, victims of narcissistic abuse may experience long-term physical health issues as a result of their abuse. These issues can include headaches, tense muscles, upset stomachs, and sleeplessness. Sometimes, in an attempt to cope with the abuse, victims may also neglect their health, adopting harmful habits like illicit drug use, smoking, drinking, and poor eating."

As he spoke, I could almost see Bhaskar's weary face, the lines of stress etched deeply into his features. His constant smoking and restless pacing seemed to be his way of dealing with the turmoil inside.

"In more extreme cases," Jai Sir continued, "the long-term consequences of narcissistic abuse can make it difficult for the victim to function in daily life and find enjoyment in it. They may struggle to maintain employment due to anxiety stemming from past trauma or feelings of inadequacy. Additionally, it can be challenging for them to establish and nurture positive connections and to grow as individuals, which can lead to feelings of loneliness and, in certain cases, suicidal thoughts."

I imagined Bhaskar's solitary walks, his silent suffering, and the heavy burden he carried.

"Oh my god!" When Jai sir was telling me all this, I was just observing Bhaskar. A clear image had formed in my mind of why he smokes so many cigarettes and why he keeps walking. I asked Jai sir, "Is there anything I can do to help him?"

"Just gradually assist him in becoming himself again. Do activities with him that remind him of his past interests. It might be wise to start working with him on whatever he was doing before meeting this abusive individual, so he can rediscover who he is and his soul. Such victims lose interest in everything usual, so never judge them or compare them with others. Listening is also a good way to help them, as they have been in a relationship where they were not allowed to speak. Whenever they tried to speak in front of their partner, they were usually avoided or interrupted, which gradually resulted in them either stopping talking or starting to talk to themselves in their mind."

"Take a break; it's impossible for you and your friend to constantly think about narcissistic abuse. It's very gloomy and melancholy! Take breaks where neither of you think about it. Take your friend out to lunch, go to the movies, go shopping, play video games, or do anything else that will divert your attention and, ideally, make you both laugh. Sometimes, beauty can be a great distraction, and showing love and respect to such a person could be a way to help them," he replied.

"Thank you so much, sir. You helped me a lot," I replied.

"No problem, just take care and call me whenever you need me. I know one or two doctors who are experts in this subject; I will talk to them and get more information," he said and hung up.

After he disconnected the call, I just kept looking at Bhaskar silently for a long time. Bhaskar would walk fast and pass by the floor and the bench on which I was sitting, without feeling anything, without seeing anything. Whenever he passed by, I felt as if someone had thrown a stone into the sea, and yet the sea remained silent and did not respond.

Bhaskar's eyes were moist, perhaps from crying or holding back tears. Whenever he walked, his hands would automatically clench into fists. His back pain was evident from the way he moved, each step a testament to his discomfort. Yet, the physical pain seemed insignificant compared to the emotional turmoil and anger simmering within him. Despite the back pain, he kept walking, his steps steady and unwavering. It was as if his mind was racing, and his feet matched that relentless pace. The turmoil in his mind propelled him forward, each step mirroring the speed of his thoughts.

I was just silently looking at him. It's not that he didn't notice me; he did, but he avoided looking at me and just kept walking. Suddenly, it started raining heavily, and we both got completely drenched in the park. But neither did he stop, nor did I stop staring at him. It must have been about 10 minutes since I was drenched in the rain, and my tears, which I had been holding back, finally found an excuse to fall from my eyes. I was losing control; my hands were trembling as I sat there on that bench, getting soaked in the rain.

"That's enough, let's go home now." I don't know what came over me, but I gently took Bhaskar's hand, feeling the cold rainwater between our fingers, and led him towards his house. He followed me without a word, his silence heavy with unspoken emotions. As we walked, the rain continued to pour, each drop mingling with the tears on my face. When we finally reached his house, I rang the bell, my heart pounding in my chest. Moments later, the door opened, and Divyasha stood there, her eyes widening in surprise.

I stormed into the house, my voice trembling with a mix of anger and concern as I yelled at Bhaskar, "You'll get sick! Don't you understand? You're out there, stubbornly walking in the rain like a little child! Forget what happened and move forward in life. Look at this child; see how much she is enduring because of you. Think about your old mother, worrying every single day for you. But no, you just keep dwelling on the past. Now go inside and change!"

I put my hands on my forehead, my voice breaking as I finished speaking, and then I just started crying. The weight of everything overwhelmed me, and I couldn't hold back the tears any longer. Seeing my distress, Divyasha rushed over and wrapped her arms around me, her own tears flowing freely. We stood there, holding each other tightly, both of us crying, sharing the pain and the burden of our emotions. It was a moment of raw vulnerability, where words were unnecessary, and the only thing that mattered was the comfort of each other's presence.

"Di, you also come inside. You're completely drenched, and you'll get sick," Divyasha said to me, her voice choked with tears. She reached out, her hands trembling, and gently pulled me towards the door. Her eyes were filled with worry and sadness, mirroring the storm raging inside me. As she hugged me tightly, I could feel her body shaking with sobs. The rain continued to pour down, but in that moment, all I could feel was the warmth of her embrace and the shared pain between us. It was a silent promise that we would face this together, no matter how difficult it got.

Bhaskar stood there, his gaze fixed on me. When Divyasha took hold of me and calmed me down, I was shocked by the look in Bhaskar's eyes. There was no emotion, no feeling—just a hollow emptiness. He stood in front of me like a statue, unmoving and unresponsive. Yet, in that emptiness, I could sense the depth of his pain. It was as if his soul was crying out, but his eyes remained silent. My heartbeat quickened, pounding in my chest. The more I looked at him, the more my heart raced, spiraling out of control. His silent suffering mirrored my own, and in that moment, I felt an overwhelming urge to reach out and pull him from the abyss he was trapped in.

Emotions, feelings, and sentiments all seemed futile to me. I was torn between suppressing my emotions and questioning what this man truly meant to me. But no matter how hard I tried, I couldn't push my feelings aside. Why? It was difficult for me to understand. Divyasha was gently shushing me, her hands tenderly wiping away my tears, but my eyes remained fixed on Bhaskar. His presence was like a magnet, drawing my gaze and my thoughts. The rain continued to pour, mingling with my tears, and the world around us seemed to blur. In that moment, everything else faded away, leaving only the silent connection between us, filled with unspoken pain and unresolved emotions.

Finally, Geeta Aunty came and took Bhaskar inside. Divyasha led me to her room, handed me a towel and some clothes, and pointed to the washroom door. "Di, change and come back. I'll make some masala tea for you," she said, before walking out of the room.

I didn't know what was going on in my mind. As I turned to go to the washroom, I paused and called out to Divyasha just before she left the room. "Please make a cup for Bhaskar too; he's gotten very wet," I said, my voice trembling with concern. She stopped and looked back at me, her eyes softening with understanding. "Of course, Di," she replied gently, "I'll make sure he gets some too." Her words were a small comfort, a reminder that we were all in this together, trying to care for each other in the midst of our pain.

Until now, I hadn't fully realized what I had done. As I changed clothes in the washroom, the moments spent in that park weighed heavily on my mind and heart, like a dark, looming rain cloud. What has happened to me? Why am I doing this? Questions swirled in my head, each one more confusing than the last. What is my relationship with Bhaskar? Why do I feel so much for him? He's my father's age, and he has a daughter who is almost my age. The confusion and emotions were overwhelming, making it hard to think clearly. The rain outside seemed to mirror the storm inside me, each drop a reminder of the turmoil I was experiencing.

Anyway, whatever has happened till now is over, I thought to myself. I decided I would go straight to my aunt's house and never come back. With this resolve, I quickly got dressed and stepped out of the washroom. Divyasha had not yet returned with the tea, so I decided to stay in her room. Out of habit, I went and sat at her study table. As I glanced around, my eyes fell on a diary lying open on the table. My heart skipped a beat when I saw the words written inside: "I love you, Bhaskar."

I couldn't stop myself and picked up the diary, curiosity getting the better of me. As I opened it, my eyes were immediately drawn to the first page, where a beautiful poem was written. The words flowed gracefully, each line filled with emotion and depth. It was clear that this diary held more than just thoughts; it was a window into Divyasha's heart and soul. The poem spoke of love, longing, and unspoken feelings, and as I read it, I felt a connection to the emotions she had poured onto the pages

To,
Bhaskar

"Tu ghum hai kahin kisi veeran jazeerey pae, tu ghum hai kahin kisi veeran jazeerey pae.

Woh to wakif nahi main kashti chalaney sae,

Lae aati nahi to tujhey kinarey sae.

Tu ghum hota jo kahin kisi gulzar main, tu ghum hota jo kahin kisi gulzar main.

Ikhtiyar rakhti hun gulon pae,

Wapas lauta daetey tujhey aur numaya kar kae"

From,
Divyasha

I had just started reading when Divyasha came in with the tea. The table was far enough away that I didn't notice her entering the room, but she saw me with her diary in my hands. Before I could read anything else, she cleared her throat and said, "Di, bad habit." Her voice was a mix of teasing and seriousness, and I felt a flush of embarrassment wash over me. I quickly closed the diary and looked up at her, trying to gauge her reaction. She set the tea down on the table and gave me a small, understanding smile, but I could see the hint of vulnerability in her eyes.

"Ohh!! Sorry," I quickly apologized, feeling a bit flustered, and gently placed her diary back on the table. I looked up at Divyasha, hoping she wasn't too upset.

She gave me a small smile, her eyes softening with understanding. "It's okay, Di,"

She came to me with the tea, placed it on the table, then picked up the diary and gently placed it in my hands. "You wanted to know what happened to my Bhaskar, why he became like this. Please read this, and if you can help me, please do," she said, her voice trembling with emotion. She folded her hands in front of me, her eyes pleading, and I could see the weight of her sorrow. My heart ached for her, and I knew that whatever was in that diary held the key to understanding Bhaskar's pain.

I immediately got up from the chair, gently took her joined hands in mine, and said, "Please don't do this, Divyasha. This is my profession. Even if you say no, I will definitely do something." I could see the relief in her eyes as I spoke. Then, without another word, I hugged her tightly, feeling her body shake with silent sobs. In that embrace, I wanted to convey all the support and strength I could offer. We stood there for a moment, holding onto each other, finding solace in our shared determination to help Bhaskar.

We both sat on the bed in her room, the atmosphere heavy with unspoken words. "You know, Di," Divyasha began, her voice soft and filled with a mix of sadness and resignation, "I realized when I was very young that my mother does not respect Bhaskar at all." Her eyes were distant, as if she was reliving those painful memories. I could see the hurt etched on her face, and it made my heart ache for her. She took a deep breath, as if gathering the strength to continue, and I reached out to hold her hand, offering silent support.

I found myself at a loss for words in this delicate situation, so I simply shook my head, letting her know I was listening. The silence between us was heavy, filled with unspoken emotions. I squeezed her hand gently, hoping to convey my support and understanding without needing to say anything. Sometimes, just being there and sharing the moment is enough.

Taking a sip of tea, she said, "Well, you will find everything in this diary, but there is one incident I couldn't write about. Di, please don't judge me. I was twelve years old when this happened, and since that day, I've seen Bhaskar breaking down every day."

Saying this, Divyasha got up from the bed, closed the door of her room, and came back to sit next to me. Her eyes were filled with a mix of fear and vulnerability, and I could sense the weight of the story she was about to share. I reached out and held her hand, giving it a reassuring squeeze, letting her know that I was there for her, ready to listen without judgment.

"We all came back after watching a movie that day. Bhaskar and I even fought over the popcorn in the theatre," she said, a slight smile appearing on her face. The happiness in her expression spoke volumes about the deep bond she shared with Bhaskar. It was a rare moment of joy amidst the pain, a glimpse into the loving relationship they had. Her smile, though brief, was a testament to the cherished memories they had created together, and it made me realize just how much Bhaskar meant to her.

"Whenever Mom saw us laughing or having fun together, I don't know what came over her. To this day, I haven't been able to understand it. Without any reason, she would start shouting at Bhaskar. Her language was so harsh that it felt like it made our ears bleed. Hearing such words from someone you love breaks your heart. I was too young to understand the depth of it at that time," she said, her voice trembling with the weight of the memories.

As she spoke, she held my hand tightly, seeking comfort and strength. I could feel the intensity of her emotions, the pain of reliving those moments. She took a deep breath and continued, her eyes filled with a mix of sorrow and determination.

"She couldn't tolerate that Bhaskar was having fun with me. The argument escalated, and as always, Mom listed all of Bhaskar's supposed faults, one after another, things he never did. Bhaskar just silently listened while driving. When we got home, I went to my room to sleep. Around 2:30 in the night, I woke up to fill my water bottle and saw Bhaskar sitting on the bed, his face turned away, while Mom was sleeping in just her undergarments. I thought maybe everything was alright, so I went back to sleep. But the next morning, the words my mother said... I still haven't been able to forget them. How could Bhaskar forget them as her husband?"

She stopped speaking, and a heavy silence filled the room. I could feel the weight of her words, the pain and confusion of a child trying to make sense of the turmoil in her family.

My curiosity had increased even more now, so I broke the silence, piercing the heavy atmosphere with my question. "What did she say?" I asked, my voice barely above a whisper.

Divyasha took a deep breath, her eyes reflecting the pain of the memory. "I feel like a prostitute when you touch me, she said things that no one should ever hear from their spouse," she began, her voice trembling. "She accused him of being worthless, of failing as a husband and a father. She said he was a burden, that he was the reason for all her unhappiness. The words were like daggers, cutting deep into his soul. I could see the hurt in his eyes, even though he tried to hide it. Those words have haunted him ever since, and I think they broke something inside him that night."

She paused, her eyes filling with tears. "I was too young to understand the full impact then, but now I see how those words have shaped his pain and his silence. It's like he's been carrying this invisible weight ever since, and it crushes him a little more each day."

The room was filled with a profound silence, the weight of her words hanging in the air. I squeezed her hand, feeling the depth of her sorrow and the strength it took to share this painful memory.

"I have never told this to anyone till now, but you have brought such different vibes," Divyasha said, her voice trembling with emotion. "I feel like telling you everything in the hope that one day you will be able to fix everything." Her eyes, glistening with unshed tears, locked onto mine, searching for understanding and solace.

As her words hung in the air, a heavy silence enveloped us. The room seemed to shrink, drawing us closer together in our shared vulnerability. I could feel the weight of her pain pressing down on my chest, making it hard to breathe. The dim light cast long shadows on the walls, mirroring the darkness of the emotions swirling within us.

Unable to hold back any longer, I felt my own tears well up and spill over. They traced hot, wet paths down my cheeks, mingling with the salty taste of sorrow. I reached out and took her hand, our fingers intertwining in a desperate grasp for comfort and connection. We cried together, our sobs echoing softly in the stillness, a poignant symphony of shared grief and unspoken words.

I didn't feel like leaving her house, but I knew I had to go. The weight of the moment pressed heavily on my heart as I gently wiped away Divyasha's tears. Her eyes, red and swollen, looked at me with a mixture of gratitude and sorrow. I held her close, feeling the tremors of her sobs against my chest, and whispered soothing words, trying to offer some semblance of comfort.

The room was filled with the lingering scent of her perfume, a delicate blend of jasmine and vanilla, which now seemed to carry a hint of melancholy. The soft glow of the evening sun filtered through the curtains, casting a warm, golden hue over everything, as if trying to wrap us in a gentle embrace.

Reluctantly, I pulled away and gave her one last reassuring smile. "I'll be back soon," I promised, my voice barely above a whisper. She nodded, her expression a fragile mask of hope and despair.

With her diary clutched tightly in my hand, I stepped out into the cool evening air. The sky was painted in shades of pink and orange, a stark contrast to the turmoil inside me. Each step away from her house felt like a betrayal, but I knew I needed to gather my thoughts and find a way to help her.

Arriving at my aunt's house, I felt a strange mix of relief and anxiety. The familiar surroundings offered a brief respite, but the weight of Divyasha's pain lingered with me. I sat down, the diary resting on my lap, its pages holding the secrets and sorrows she had entrusted to me. I took a deep breath, ready to delve into her world and find a way to bring her the peace she so desperately needed.

Sarika Di was still sleeping and Aunt and Uncle had also gone to their job. I came back from Divyasha's house and sat on the sofa there. My mind was telling me to stop but I don't know why my heart was repeatedly telling me to let whatever was happening happen. That diary was kept in front of me but I don't know why I could not gather the courage to read it. There was a fear in my mind which was stopping me again and again. But finally, I started reading it.

To,
Bhaskar
Dear Diary

These pages provide me with comfort and protection from the storms raging in our home. My mother, Ayesha Dhillon, is a storm – a natural force that leaves nothing but damage and destruction in its wake. Her greatness is mostly focused on my father Bhaskar, because her narcissism problem has gripped him.

Bhaskar's eyes, once warm, are now moist as if reflecting the parched sky. His shoulders have sagged due to Ayesha's constant guilt-tripping of him. She brags about her professional achievements, dominance over colleagues, and excellent cooking. But it's all a ruse - a frantic attempt to fill the emptiness within.

Every time Bhaskar tries to free himself from her shadow, she tries harder to enslave him. Bhaskar's eyes are fixed on the hazy memories of the time when love flowed between them and now he is a prisoner in his own house. Ayesha's overestimation of her strength prevents her from realizing his pain. She considers his problems as weakness.

The sounds of their laughter would echo through the halls of their Delhi home at that time. Bhaskar would surprise Ayesha with handwritten messages written in her favorite novels. She would blush with embarrassment, her pretentious self-importance temporarily forgotten. They were partners, equals, two souls entangled in the dance of existence.

But now Bhaskar's gaze is fixed on those frozen seconds. His fingers trace the features of Ayesha's face, etched in sepia tones. He wonders how they got here, where love has faded and been replaced by the cold grip of Ayesha's narcissism.

Ayesha, too busy with her own achievements, constantly dismisses Bhaskar's achievements and problems. His mental health is deteriorating, yet she calls it weakness. "You're lucky you have me," she says, her voice hard as glass. "I've sacrificed a lot for this family." But what about the invisible sacrifices, etched on Bhaskar's aching heart?

He therefore goes deeper into the sea of his memories, delving deeper into old letters and forgotten poems, searching for answers to these seemingly impossible questions. Ayesha sees Bhaskar's etched phrases, once vows of love, now as mere artifacts. Bhaskar yearns for the warmth of Ayesha's touch and the belief that he is important despite his unremarkable exterior.

Bhaskar's silence grows more pronounced over time. He clings to memories, believing they will help him ride out the storm. But Ayesha blinds him to his suffering by overestimating her powers. She is the captain of a sinking ship, unaware of the leaks below deck.

As a result, Bhaskar suffers silently like a prisoner of a terrible love. Slowly the walls of the room absorb his tears where Bhaskar had imagined some happy moments that were elevated above any kind of ego and self-importance, and today those clichéd fantasies stand testimony to a love that was once soaring but is now struggling to breathe.

From,
Divyasha
With love

After reading everything, my mind, which had been in turmoil, finally settled. I decided to call my dad and share everything about Bhaskar. Hearing my words, he too became upset, but he gave his approval for my first case. He said, "Niharika, I have faith in you. You have the ability to turn a barren field into a flourishing garden. Just go for it. I am with you, no matter what."

These words of Papa aroused enthusiasm in me and I directly called Jai Sir.

"Hello, sir!"

"Hello Niharika" he replied

"Sir, Can you please guide me about how to start treating a person who is suffering from narcissist abuse?" I asked

"Psychodynamic therapy is an important tool for helping people recover from narcissistic abuse. Remember that recovering from narcissistic abuse is a process, and therapy provides a personalized path to regaining one's sense of self and resilience. Seeking the help of a skilled therapist specializing in trauma and narcissistic abuse reintegration is an important step in the process." Jai sir said in a tone of praise to me.

"All right sir, thank you very much, bye" I said

"Bye Niharika, this will not be easy but I have faith in you, you will definitely succeed" Jai Sir motivated me and disconnected the call

I have always been fascinated by the human mind's complex structure. As a psychology student, I was involved by the subtle dance between conscious and unconscious thinking. But I had no idea that my trip into the depths of the psyche would take me to a crossroads of healing and forbidden feelings.

Bhaskar faced life's storms. His eyes spoke stories of lost love, abandoned hopes, and hidden scars. I observed him amid the intense downpour, his eyes fixed on the flashing raindrops. I was curious about the shadows he carried, the echoes of agony engraved onto his features.

As luck would have it, my curiosity brought me to Bhaskar's door. Offering to listen and explore the contours of his thinking. The therapist's chair will become our shared refuge, a place where words will pour like monsoon rain, healing early scars.

The weight of Ayesha's narcissistic grasp and her inflated sense of self-importance overpowered him, leaving hidden scars that ran deep. Each interaction with her was like a storm, eroding his sense of self bit by bit. They probed the consequences through open discourse and introspection, uncovering the profound impact on Bhaskar—the loss of his identity, the remnants of a man who once believed in love and now struggled to find his place in the world.

Divyasha, Bhaskar's daughter, noticed the difference. She, too, felt the oppressive weight of her mother's narcissism, a constant shadow over their lives. Her decision to separate Bhaskar from Ayesha was an act of profound love, a desperate attempt to free him from the invisible chains that bound him. It was a courageous move, driven by the hope of seeing her father reclaim his lost sense of self.

As I observed them, I understood the subtle agreement between daughter and father, the unspoken promise of healing. Their eyes would meet, and in those brief moments, a silent understanding passed between them—a shared resolve to mend the broken pieces of their lives. The air was thick with unvoiced emotions, a blend of pain and hope that hung heavily around them.

Divyasha's actions were a testament to her strength and compassion, a beacon of light in the midst of their turmoil. She was determined to see her father rise above the wreckage of his past, to help him find the man he once was. And in that quiet, unspoken bond, there was a glimmer of hope for a brighter future.

It must have been around 2 o'clock in the afternoon when I fell asleep on the couch, my mind swirling with thoughts of Bhaskar. The room was quiet, the only sound the faint ticking of a clock, as I drifted into a restless sleep.

I was awakened around 5 in the evening by Sarika Di. The soft light of the setting sun filtered through the curtains, casting a warm glow across the room. Sarika Di had learned everything that had transpired that morning.

She gently shook me awake and handed me a steaming cup of coffee, the rich aroma filling the air.

With a teasing smile, she said, "Have you come here for my wedding or to find your first case?" Her words were lighthearted, but her eyes held a depth of understanding and concern. I took the coffee, feeling the warmth seep into my hands, and managed a small smile in return. The weight of the day's events still lingered, but her presence and the simple act of sharing a cup of coffee brought a moment of comfort and clarity.

I was at a loss for words, so I simply looked at her with a confused expression and returned to sipping my coffee. The warmth of the mug was comforting, but my mind was still a whirlwind of thoughts and emotions.

Sarika Di noticed my confusion and gently patted me on the back. "Look," she said with a reassuring smile, "you just have to dance at the wedding. The rest is handled by an event organizer." Her words were meant to lighten the mood, and I could see the concern in her eyes.

She then came closer, took the coffee mug from my hands, and placed it on the table. The gesture was simple, yet it conveyed her care and understanding. I felt a bit more at ease, knowing that she was there to support me through this chaotic time.

She held my hand, her grip firm yet gentle, and said, "Please cure Bhaskar uncle; I can't bear to see the pain of that girl. Divyasha had come to return your clothes; she told me how today you saved uncle from getting wet in the rain."

I sighed deeply, feeling the weight of her plea. "Di, yes, I had talked to Jai sir before sleeping. Jai Sir says that narcissistic abuse is very critical and its victim has to be treated very gently. It is not possible for me to solve such a complex case." The words felt heavy on my tongue, a mix of frustration and helplessness.

Saying this, I walked over to the window and stood there, staring out at the world beyond. The sky was a canvas of fading light, the colors blending into a soft twilight. The cool evening breeze brushed against my face, a small comfort amidst the turmoil inside me. I felt Sarika Di's presence behind me, a silent support, as I tried to gather my thoughts and find a way forward.

To understand the pain of this helplessness, I looked out the window and saw Bhaskar and Divyasha standing together. The sight brought a soothing sensation to my eyes, a gentle balm to my aching heart. The pang of emotion went straight to my core, filling me with a renewed sense of purpose.

I turned towards Sarika Di, my resolve firm. "Whatcvcr happens, I will make Bhaskar happy again," I said, my voice steady with determination. The promise hung in the air, a vow to bring light back into their lives despite the challenges ahead.

CHAPTER TWO

Dear Diary

To,
Bhaskar
Dear Diary

Bhaskar lies alone on this hopeless island, cut off from both love and mental balance. The narcissist's web has gripped him, and the world seems as isolated as a hazy memory. Bhaskar is the only one who lives on this rocky shore, and his heart aches with loneliness.

The narcissistic remark has etched itself into Bhaskar's psyche like a coral. He looks at his reflection in the dirty water and finds himself distorted and shattered. Who is he today? The waves mock him, destroying his self-consciousness.

The gust of wind whispers the disappointing and bitter words uttered by the self-absorbed wife to Bhasker. 'You are worthless,' she mutters. 'Nobody cares.' Bhasker clutches his chest, feeling the impact of each insult. My mother's voice echoes in the hollows of his mind.

Maybe a ship will come along, and a rescuer will take him away. Hope, however, is a fragile boat, and the horizon remains barren. I want to connect with someone who can see his wounds as he is held captive on an island that not only holds him captive but also sucks away like a leech in the hope of fulfilling his unfulfilled dreams.

My mother's arrogant betrayal has left Bhaskar stranded on an island from which it seems impossible to get out without help. He is now afraid of companionship, he has lost the ability to feel anyone's company and now he only enjoys the taste of loneliness. Seeing him in this state, I feel that he has created a hidden agenda in his mind in which he has become a lighthouse keeper himself, instructing ships to stay away and telling them that solitude is better than more destruction.

Loneliness is Bhasker's only friend now, but it's a strange feeling that brings him nothing but misery every day. He wants solitude because he is hurt by my mother's harsh voice which is like these sharp rocks. Will someone ever come and bring Bhaskar out of these sharp rocks and bring him to me smiling like he used to be before?

Sometimes, in Bhaskar's footprints, imaginary marks of my mother's harshness appear. Bhaskar is troubled by these painful memories. I wonder if anyone else will ever walk alongside him and leave gentle marks.

Bhaskar still collects wood that has drifted into the flowing sea of emptiness and builds a makeshift house that collapses with the slightest blow. Survival has become his mantra, perhaps in the hope that one day he will find the love he lost because of my mother's narcissistic behavior. But the seawater weakens his resolve. How long can he endure this desolation? How long will he be lost in the darkness?

Bhaskar's island of love remains a silent testimony to his plight. The waves continue their relentless assault, eroding and changing the shoreline of his feelings of love every day.

From,
Divyasha.
With love

The words Divyasha had written in her diary gave me goosebumps. When Sarika Di invited me to her wedding in Ajmer, I saw it as a chance to escape the hustle and bustle of Delhi and immerse myself in a different environment. Little did I know that this journey would change my life forever.

Now, my world had taken a different turn, one filled with darkness. There were people who could show the way, but even they were unaware of where this path would lead. It felt as if the silence in the dark alley was persistently trying to scare me, repeatedly telling me not to venture down this ominous path. Yet, Bhaskar's eyes gave me courage, and Divyasha's affection and trust encouraged me to move forward.

Thinking about all these things, I felt a headache coming on. I rummaged through my bag for a headache pill and noticed a sexy, above-knee-length dress I had brought for Sarika Di's bachelor party. Jai Sir's words echoed in my mind: beauty can be a good way to connect with a narcissistic victim.

With renewed determination, I quickly put on the dress and did some light makeup. The transformation gave me a boost of confidence. I hoped that presenting myself this way might help Bhaskar open up and share his thoughts, making it easier for me to understand him.

With a mix of nerves and hope, I headed straight to Bhaskar's house. The evening air was cool against my skin, and each step felt like a step closer to breaking through the walls that had been built around his heart. I knocked on the door, ready to face whatever lay ahead, hoping that tonight would be the night he would finally speak and let me in.

I rang the bell, and as usual, Divyasha opened the door. I greeted her casually with a "hi," and she invited me inside. We both sat in the drawing room, the familiar surroundings offering a sense of comfort. The room was filled with the soft hum of the ceiling fan and the faint aroma of incense lingering in the air.

Divyasha quickly excused herself and ran to the kitchen to get water for me. As I waited, my eyes couldn't help but wander, searching for any sign of Bhaskar. I tried to peek inside the house discreetly, hoping to catch a glimpse of him. The anticipation made my heart race slightly, each moment feeling like an eternity.

The drawing room was cozy, with family photos adorning the walls and a soft, worn-out sofa that invited you to sink into its cushions. Despite the warmth of the room, my thoughts were solely focused on Bhaskar, hoping that today would be the day he would open up and share his thoughts with me.

When she came back with a glass of water, I asked, "I can't see Bhaskar. Has he gone out for a walk again?"

"No, he has fallen sick because of getting wet in the rain; he is sleeping inside his room," she replied, her voice tinged with concern.

"Ohhh, I wish I could have brought him home a little sooner. Can I meet him?" I asked, hoping for a chance to see him.

"He doesn't talk to anyone, so there's no point in meeting him," she replied, her tone resigned.

"Can you tell me anything more specific about him that could help me understand him? Actually, I talked to my teacher about Bhaskar, and he said that it is very difficult to cure narcissistic victims because they are completely broken from inside," I said, trying to gather more insights.

"You are right, Didi, but I have a lot of faith in you. I have consulted many doctors in Delhi and Ajmer, but no one understood his emotions like you did from the very first day. That is why I have more faith in you," she said, her voice filled with urgency and pressure.

"Have you ever taken Bhaskar out for a walk?" I asked her, hoping to find a way to connect with him.

"Yes, many times, but it has been of no use. He just goes out and comes back without having any fun or talking much. Once, in anger, I shouted at him, 'What is your problem? We don't even live with that woman anymore, so why do you live like a living dead?' But he placed his hand on my head and said, 'I don't feel like doing anything. I am scared. Please leave me alone.'" She recounted this with a very heavy heart, her voice trembling with emotion.

I got up and stood near the window, the cool breeze brushing against my face. "I want to meet Bhaskar right now," I said, turning around and walking back to Divyasha with determination.

"I have a plan, but I need your support. Look, I wore this dress for Bhaskar because, according to Jai Sir, victims can be cured through beauty. They have suppressed their feelings for years, and those feelings have now become wounds. Just like iron cuts iron, only beauty can heal the wound caused by beauty," I explained, my voice steady and hopeful.

Divyasha looked at me, her eyes wide with a mix of surprise and curiosity. I could see the wheels turning in her mind as she processed my words. The room was filled with a tense anticipation, the air thick with the weight of our shared mission. I reached out and gently squeezed her hand, seeking her support and understanding.

"What's the plan, Di?" she asked, her curiosity piqued.

"Come on, get him ready. Let's go out somewhere," I said, my voice filled with determination.

"Where will we go? He won't agree so easily," she replied, a hint of doubt in her voice.

"Where does he feel most at ease?" I asked, hoping to find a place that would make him comfortable.

"Maybe the park," she suggested, offering an option.

"Cool, let's go," I said, feeling a surge of hope.

Divyasha nodded and quickly went to get Bhaskar ready. The anticipation was palpable as we prepared to take this crucial step. The park, with its serene environment and open spaces, seemed like the perfect place to help Bhaskar start opening up. I hoped that this outing would be the beginning of his healing journey.

Divyasha was also very excited, so we both went to Bhaskar's room and started insisting that he come to the park with us. One by one, we both pressured him to join us for a walk. But all our efforts were in vain; he just kept lying on the bed with his face turned away, not even glancing in our direction. Exhausted and disheartened, we returned to the drawing room.

"I told you earlier that it wouldn't be that easy," Divyasha stated, a hint of frustration in her voice. Then, with a small smile, she added, "By the way, you look really beautiful in this dress."

I sighed, feeling a mix of gratitude and disappointment. "But what's the benefit if Bhaskar didn't even see it? Thank you, though. You're really sweet. If I ever have a daughter, I pray to God that she will be just like you," I said, giving her a warm smile. Then, rubbing my temples, I asked, "Do you have any pills for a headache?"

"Bhaskar gave you a headache too, right?" she said with a small, knowing smile as she opened a medical box on the nearby table and handed me a pill.

As I took the medicine from her, I asked, "Why do you call your father by name?"

Divyasha sighed deeply before continuing, her voice tinged with sadness. "He was always so loving and free-spirited. He never imposed his wishes on anyone, and my mother took advantage of this. Whenever she needed something, she would speak to him sweetly, and Bhaskar would fall into her trap easily. But whenever he needed her, she would accuse him of something or blame him for past issues. She would insult him, mock his innocence, and belittle his love."

She paused, her eyes reflecting the pain of those memories. "I remember very well the day when Bhaskar wanted to come to Ajmer to take care of grandfather. Mother fought with him forcefully and insulted him over every little thing. It was heartbreaking to see."

Her words painted a vivid picture of the emotional turmoil Bhaskar had endured, and it was clear how deeply it had affected both him and Divyasha. The bond they shared, despite the hardships, was evident in the way she spoke about him.

"She used to say that raising the child is not my sole responsibility. I earn more than you. I am in a good position in my job and you are still struggling. That is why your job does not matter. If I work for longer hours, my income is also that much. You work for longer hours and can hardly cover your commuting expenses," Divyasha recounted, her voice growing more intense with each word.

As she spoke, her eyes darkened with anger, and her hands clenched into fists. "Bhaskar had to leave his job because my mother did not want him to go out. She lovingly asked him to leave the job one day, and then, after a few days, she started accusing Bhaskar of not doing any work. Her style of talking was so manipulative that Bhaskar started feeling he was incapable of doing anything."

Her voice trembled with suppressed rage, and her face flushed with emotion. "She made him feel worthless, like he couldn't do anything right. It was heartbreaking to watch him lose his confidence and sense of self-worth."

The room seemed to vibrate with the intensity of her emotions, the air thick with the weight of her words. It was clear how deeply her mother's actions had scarred both Bhaskar and Divyasha, leaving lasting wounds that were still raw and painful.

I felt like stopping her and controlling her a bit, but I wanted to know more, so I thought it was not appropriate to interrupt her at this time. So I kept listening to everything quietly.

"She is not only clever; she knows how to mislead people very well. She has used me as a weapon to mislead Bhaskar many times. I was very young and couldn't do anything at that time, but now, as long as I am alive, I will never let her do this again. Bhaskar kept yearning for me, forgetting all his happiness, and today, see what has happened to him—he has become just a living corpse."

Her voice broke, and she started crying, tears streaming down her face.

Her pain was palpable, and I could see the deep scars left by her mother's manipulations. I wanted to reach out and comfort her, but I knew she needed to let it all out. The room was filled with her sobs, a raw and heartbreaking sound that echoed the years of suffering and helplessness she had endured.

She was not the only one crying; I was right there with her, my own tears refusing to stop. Honestly, I felt an overwhelming urge to run to Bhaskar, to hug him and cry together, but that wasn't possible.

Today, I found myself lost in a whirlwind of thoughts, trapped in a turbulence of imagination. These imaginations broke the boundaries of reality, blurring the lines between what is and what could be. It's fascinating how our minds create complex stories, especially when reality feels like a labyrinth. Dreams linger, but reality draws closer. Bhaskar's eyes are tired, and Ayesha's laughter seems hollow.

Divyasha is the keeper of their secrets; she holds their emotions in her delicate mind, the link between two worlds. Perhaps, I can rewrite Bhaskar's story in a way that respects and honors his feelings. The thought gave me a glimmer of hope amidst the chaos, a belief that maybe, just maybe, I could help bring light back into their lives.

Maybe I should go home now. Maybe my presence is only adding to Divyasha's pain. I am just a 23-year-old young girl. No matter what I do, I can't make Bhaskar the same as before. I left Divyasha in the same condition and started to leave, but seeing her cry like that, my pity for Bhaskar turned into anger. I turned around and went to Bhaskar's room, determined to confront him.

I sat beside him and spoke very lovingly but firmly. "You don't care for your daughter at all, do you? She cries every day seeing you in this state, but no, your grief is too great. You can't even laugh. Her happiness has gone to hell, and you just keep crying and making your daughter cry. If you had to live like this, then why did you leave Ayesha and come with her? You would have stayed with her till death. Who are we? What do we mean to you that you would care for us? Have you ever thought about what Divyasha's dreams are, what she wants to do in life, and what she wants to become? You just lie in your room like a dead person or roam around with a cigarette in your mouth."

After saying all this, I felt a mix of frustration and sadness. I left Bhaskar's room and went back to my aunt's house, hoping that my words might spark something in him.

After coming back from Bhaskar's house, I hugged Sarika Di tightly and started crying bitterly. "Di, what is all this happening? Why is it happening? Why am I feeling so bad for Bhaskar? After all, what does he mean to me that I forget everything and keep getting drawn towards him every time?" I poured out my heart to her as soon as I hugged her.

I had now included Sarika Di in the storm that was raging in my heart. She probably knew me better than I knew myself. She patted my back gently, her touch soothing my frayed nerves.

"Don't panic and keep quiet," she said softly. "Your age is such that it is normal to have such feelings. Yes, you will have to learn to control these feelings, otherwise things can get really messed up. Now sit back and tell me what's going on."

Her calm and understanding demeanor provided a much-needed anchor in the emotional tempest I was experiencing. I took a deep breath, trying to steady myself, and began to recount everything that had happened, hoping that sharing my burden would help me find some clarity.

I told Didi while sobbing, my voice trembling with emotion, "Ever since the day I saw Bhaskar, I have not slept properly. He is on my mind all the time. I am worried about him constantly. Why?"

Didi looked at me with a gentle, understanding smile, her eyes filled with empathy. "Bhaskar uncle is handsome, and you have just become a young woman, so there is no harm in being a little attracted to him. The problem is when you can't stay away from him and you only like him. So now, to solve your problem, we are going to the club today. You are already dressed, so touch up quickly. I will also come after getting ready."

She got up gracefully and started changing, her movements fluid and confident. I wiped my tears and began touching up my makeup, which was smudged and ruined from crying. My hands were shaking slightly, but I took a deep breath and focused on the task.

It was going to take at least an hour for Didi to get ready, so I decided to pass the time by reading Divyasha's diary. The thought of diving into someone else's world, even for a little while, felt like a small escape from my own swirling emotions.

To,
Bhaskar,
Dear Diary

My mother, Ayesha Dhillon, is a complex woman, a mix of elegance and ferocity. She is now fifty-three, but her narcissistic disorder has gotten worse with age. It is like a poison that seeps into our lives, destroying everything it touches. Today, I find myself torn between love and despair.

With her obvious superiority complex, my mother flaunts her accomplishments at work, her designer wardrobe, and her perfect taste, but in private she's a dictator who feeds off power, believing she's special and selected by some cosmic force to rise above the others.

In her view, she is the sun, and we are simply planets orbiting around her. She wants adoration, loyalty, and unflinching attention; anybody who questions her dominance suffers her fury, including my father, Bhaskar.

Bhaskar, likewise 53, is a delicate soul. His affection for my mom has endured storms, however recently, it's turned into a twister. His psychological wellness weakens every day.

Ayesha's cutting comments, her regard for his weakness — these injuries putrefy. He's a detainee in his own home, and I can't tolerate watching him endure.

Today, I made a decision: I took Bhaskar away from Ayesha. We quietly packed his belongings, to escape her clutches. While leaving the house, Bhaskar's trembling hands held my hands, which were once full of fun, but now filled with sadness. We arrived in Ajmer, a city of beautiful hills, where the scent of freedom was in the air.

I am writing this in the dim light of my home in Ajmer. Bhaskar is sitting near the window and looking at the raindrops. His once dynamic eyes have now become fearful. I promise myself that I will save him, save him from Ayesha's poison. But, how can you save someone from his own wife? This fear haunts me every day but I still have faith that one day someone will come who will teach my Bhaskar to laugh again.

I know what is going to happen; Ayesha will lose her temper with me. She will call me ungrateful and accuse me of betrayal. But I will not let her hurt Bhaskar anymore. He deserves compassion, love, and peace - all of which Ayesha denies.

I have been reading about love languages; I believe Ayesha's language is "acts of service" because she wants everyone to meet her needs, while Bhaskar's language is "words of affirmation" because he needs to be accepted. As for me, I am trying to reassure Bhaskar by spending quality time with him, which Bhaskar has been waiting for so long because my mother has done nothing but curse and insult him.

Even if it means confronting the woman who gave birth to me, Diary, I will fight for Bhaskar and be his shield. Perhaps love can heal the wounds inflicted by Ayesha, or perhaps it is time to break all ties.

From,
Divyasha
With love

The things Divyasha had written in that diary were tearing my mind apart. Each word felt like a dagger, twisting deeper into my tangled emotions. My brain felt like it was losing its light, drowning in a sea of confusion and heartache. Thank God Di came; if I had thought about Bhaskar for even 10 more minutes, I would have gone crazy.

"Let's go, how do I look?" Sarika Di asked, her voice breaking through my chaotic thoughts. She stood there, looking radiant and confident, but I was still stuck between the haunting words of Divyasha and the overwhelming presence of Bhaskar.

"Sister, should we take Divyasha along as well?" I asked, my voice barely above a whisper, still lost in my turmoil.

"You have completely lost your mind, Niharika! She's still a kid. Come on, the cab is here now," Sarika Di almost scolded me, her tone sharp but laced with concern. Her words jolted me back to reality, and I realized how absurd my suggestion had been.

Finally, we arrived at the club with Di's friends, a lively group consisting of two boys and four girls, including me and Di. The moment we stepped inside, the pulsating music and vibrant lights enveloped us. I immediately grabbed a beer, hoping to drown out the incessant thoughts of Bhaskar that plagued my mind.

Both boys were strikingly handsome, young, and most importantly, they were my age. One of them, with a charming smile, asked me for a dance. I didn't hesitate and we made our way to the dance floor. He moved with such grace and confidence, his dancing skills quickly captivating all the girls, including me. His name was Siddharth, and he had a magnetic presence that was hard to ignore.

After dancing for about two minutes, I returned to the table and sat down with Sarika Di. She looked at me with a knowing smile and asked, "Are you having fun?"

"Yes, sister, I am having a lot of fun. Bhaskar really dances very well," I blurted out, not realizing my slip. Embarrassed, I quickly downed the entire mug of beer on the table and hurried back to the dance floor, trying to escape my own awkwardness.

We danced for hours, the music and the alcohol blurring the lines of time. Eventually, we made our way back home. I was completely unconscious, having drunk far too much. The last thing I remembered was the comforting darkness of sleep overtaking me.

When I woke up, Sarika Di was staring at me with an intense, almost accusatory look. "What happened,

Di? Why are you looking at me as if I have stolen your husband?" I started laughing loudly, thinking I had cracked a good joke. But Di's worried expression didn't change, so I quickly fell silent.

"Did I do something wrong by drinking last night? Please tell me, Di, I'm getting tense now seeing you so silent," I said, holding my head as it throbbed with a painful hangover.

"Not my husband, but maybe you are trying to steal someone else's husband," Sarika Di said, gripping my shoulders firmly.

"Whose?" I asked, confusion clouding my mind.

"Stupid girl, you were chanting Bhaskar's name the whole night," Di said, shaking my shoulders vigorously. Her words hit me like a cold splash of water, and I felt a wave of embarrassment wash over me.

"Come to your senses," Di said, her voice sharp and commanding.

"I came to my senses," I replied, trying to sound confident but feeling a knot of anxiety tightening in my stomach.

"You are not in your senses because of the intoxication of alcohol but because of this new intoxication of love that has taken over your head," Di said, her eyes piercing through me with a mix of frustration and concern.

"What are you saying?" I asked, my voice trembling slightly.

"You were saying Bhaskar's name the whole night and you even kissed me. It was fine till that time, but then you climbed on top of me. I had to sleep on the floor the whole night," Di said, standing up from the bed with an exasperated sigh.

Her words hit me like a ton of bricks. I felt a wave of shame and confusion wash over me. I couldn't believe what I had done. The room seemed to spin as I tried to process her words, my head still throbbing from the hangover.

"What are you talking about? I don't remember anything," I said shyly, feeling a deep sense of embarrassment.

"I am sorry, Di," I added, holding my ears in a gesture of apology.

"It's not about your sorry, Niharika, or what you did to me, but it's about what you are going to do to yourself," Di said, coming closer. She patted my cheeks gently, her touch warm and reassuring. "From today onwards, you will not meet anyone, neither Divyasha nor Bhaskar."

"But why?" I asked, confusion and worry evident in my voice.

"Because I think you have fallen in love with Bhaskar uncle," Di spoke nervously, her eyes searching mine for understanding.

"Haha, and why do you think so?" I asked, trying to laugh it off, but my heart was pounding in my chest.

Didi shouted at me, her voice filled with frustration and concern, "Because I am three years older than you! Don't forget that my love marriage is happening in a few days, and you have come to attend my wedding. Also, don't forget that Bhaskar is 30 years older than you!"

"There is nothing like that, you are getting worried for no reason," I said, trying to sound nonchalant, but deep inside, I knew something was wrong with me. My heart was heavy with confusion and unspoken feelings.

"I am going out with your brother-in-law, and you promise me that you will neither meet Divyasha nor think anything about Bhaskar uncle," she told me firmly, her eyes locking onto mine, demanding a promise. Then she left, leaving me alone with a whirlwind of questions and incomplete answers.

CHAPTER THREE

Inebriation

Today started off weirdly, and I couldn't shake the uneasy feeling. After Di's stern words, I decided to take a bath, hoping the cold water would wash away my confusion. As I stood under the shower, I realized Di was right—I had been thinking too much about Bhaskar. This was the perfect time to stop.

Determined to clear my mind, I decided that I would not dwell on anything else. My first step was to return Divyasha's diary. It felt like a symbolic gesture, a way to let go of the tangled emotions and start fresh.

But my heart had overpowered my mind. While bathing, I couldn't help but remember that rainy day when I was sitting on the bench in the park, watching Bhaskar as he walked by. The memory of that moment brought a strange pleasure, and with my eyes closed, I started touching my body without even wanting to. It felt as if fire was emanating from my skin.

It wasn't the first time I had touched myself, but I had never felt so complete before today. The thought of Bhaskar created a tingling sensation throughout my body, as if I had discovered the very purpose of my existence. The intensity of my feelings was overwhelming, and I realized just how deeply he had affected me.

I wanted to come to my senses, but the feeling was so sweet that I felt helpless, unable to resist. The water from the shower cascaded over my body, and it felt like a volcano had erupted within me. I tried to bring myself back to consciousness, but my eyes refused to open until this volcano had fully erupted.

My heartbeat raced beyond limits, and in my mind, I hugged Bhaskar tightly in nervousness. A voice in my head kept whispering, "Just stay in my embrace for a little longer." Finally, the moment came when I forgot the whole world and drowned myself in the sigh of my own breath, completely lost in the intensity of my emotions.

This journey of inebriation was now at its peak and with a shiver, my hands stopped. Now I remained in this position for some time enjoying the rain from the shower. My mind was telling me that I should feel bad, but my heart had decided not to listen to my mind.

I came out of the bath, put on my clothes, picked up Divyasha's diary, and went straight to her house to return it. When I rang the bell, I expected Divyasha to open the door as usual. But today, it seemed as if fate had decided to play a trick on me. When the door opened, there stood Bhaskar, wearing a sleeveless T-shirt and shorts. I was taken aback by how incredibly attractive he looked, even at his age.

He greeted me with a casual "hi" and invited me inside. My heart raced as I stepped into the house. In the drawing room, I saw Divyasha sitting and reading something. I could hardly believe my eyes. The man who had barely acknowledged me yesterday was now opening the door himself and inviting me in.

I stepped inside, my eyes wide with surprise, and gestured to Divyasha, silently asking what had happened to Bhaskar. She was so overjoyed to see me that it felt like a miracle had appeared before her. Without wasting any time, she grabbed my hand and pulled me straight to her room.

"Didi, you have done a miracle that no doctor, no therapist has been able to do till date. You did it in two days! Didi, you are not just my sister, you are a godsend," she exclaimed, her eyes shining with gratitude. She moved towards me and started kissing my forehead repeatedly.

I felt a warm glow inside, still in shock at how all this had happened because of me. I hadn't done anything, or so I thought. When Divyasha finally stopped kissing my forehead, she held me by the shoulders, made me sit on the bed, and started saying, "Thank you."

I stopped Divyasha in the middle, calming her down and asking, "Tell me what happened."

"Did you see Bhaskar?" she asked, her eyes wide with excitement.

"Yes, I noticed some changes too, but how did this happen and what is my contribution in all this?" I asked, still puzzled.

"That day when you went to explain things to Bhaskar, after you left, he came to me and placed his hand on my head. He said, 'Forgive me, daughter. I had become very negative and couldn't understand what you must be going through because of my actions. But today, I promise you that I will forget my past life and move forward only for you.'"

She hugged me tightly as she recounted the moment, her voice filled with emotion. I felt a surge of warmth and pride, realizing that my words had somehow sparked a positive change in Bhaskar. It was a moment of unexpected joy and relief, knowing that things were starting to look up for Divyasha and her father.

"I wanted to come to you and tell you everything, but I stopped, thinking that you would be so surprised when you see all this yourself," she exclaimed, her eyes sparkling with excitement. As she finished speaking, she began to jump up and down like a child who had just discovered a hidden treasure, her laughter echoing through the room. Her movements were wild and unrestrained, her joy so palpable that it seemed to fill the air around her.

Absolutely! The anticipation of something she has been eagerly waiting for years would undoubtedly bring her immense joy. It's like the culmination of all her dreams and efforts finally coming to fruition. The excitement and happiness she feels are completely natural and well-deserved.

"Divyasha, come out, grandma has made pasta for you, and bring your friend too," Bhaskar called out. The moment his words reached our ears, Divyasha and I couldn't contain our excitement. We looked at each other with wide, gleaming eyes and, without a second thought, started dancing around her room. Our laughter filled the air as we twirled and jumped, our joy as infectious as a child's on a festive morning. The promise of grandma's delicious pasta was enough to turn the room into our little dance floor, where happiness knew no bounds.

As we danced our way into the drawing room, our laughter echoing through the house, we finally collapsed onto the couch, still giggling. In that moment, I felt like a child again, swept up in the pure joy of the moment. Despite being only three years older than Divyasha, I found myself reveling in the fun just as much as she was. It was as if the years between us melted away, leaving only the shared happiness of two friends enjoying a simple, delightful moment together.

Bhaskar brought the steaming bowls of pasta to the table, the delicious aroma filling the room. As he placed them in front of us, he looked at me with a grateful smile and said, "Thank you, Niharika, for making me realize that I am not alone. I have my daughter with me and my old mother too, whom I have to take care of." His words were filled with warmth and sincerity, and I could see the relief and newfound purpose in his eyes. It was a touching moment, one that made the simple act of sharing a meal feel incredibly special.

"And I, I am also with you," I said softly, my voice trailing off as I suddenly felt a wave of uncertainty. Had I overstepped? But before I could dwell on it, Divyasha chimed in with a bright smile, "Yes Bhaskar, Di is there too." Her words were like a warm embrace, reassuring me that my presence was valued. Bhaskar's eyes softened, and a gentle smile spread across his face, making the moment feel even more special. It was a simple affirmation, but it carried so much warmth and connection.

Bhaskar started walking away, his laughter echoing softly in the room. Suddenly, I felt an urge to say something more, and before I knew it, I shouted, "Bhaskar!" My voice rang out, and I immediately fell silent, unsure of what to say next. He turned around, a gentle smile playing on his lips, and responded warmly, "Yes, Niharika?" His eyes held a mix of curiosity and kindness, making me feel both nervous and comforted at the same time.

I felt a warm flutter in my heart, wishing that Bhaskar would keep calling my name, and I could just listen to his voice forever. Just then, Geeta Aunty, Bhaskar's mother, walked in. She gently caressed my cheek, her touch filled with affection. "Live long, daughter," she said, her voice brimming with gratitude. "Because of you, after so many years, this house has become vibrant again. May God fulfill all your wishes." Her words were like a blessing, wrapping me in a cocoon of warmth and love. It was a moment of pure, heartfelt connection that made me feel truly cherished.

Geeta Aunty's hand gently touched my head, her fingers weaving through my hair with a tenderness that felt like a soothing lullaby. It was as if time slowed down, and I could imagine myself sinking into her lap, the world fading away as I drifted into a peaceful slumber. In that moment, a wave of pure happiness washed over me, a joy so profound that it eclipsed even the pride I felt when I cleared my entrance test. The sight of this family, their laughter filling the room, brought a warmth to my heart that I hadn't felt in years. It was a simple, yet deeply cherished moment, one that reminded me of the beauty of genuine human connection.

But this serene moment shattered like glass when my phone rang, jolting me back to reality. It was Sarika Di calling. I reluctantly moved aside and answered. The urgency in her voice was palpable as she immediately asked, "You are at home, right? You haven't gone to Divyasha's place." Her words hung in the air, casting a sudden shadow over the warmth I had just felt.

I said hesitantly, "No, I am at home. What happened?"

"Good girl," she replied with a hint of relief in her voice. "I am coming home in a while, and your brother-in-law is also with me. You also get ready. We are all going to watch a movie." With that, Di disconnected the call, leaving me standing there, the warmth of the previous moment now mingling with a new sense of anticipation.

I quickly ran to Divyasha, handing her the diary that lay on the table. I planted a quick kiss on her cheek, feeling the warmth of our bond in that brief moment. Then, I touched Geeta Aunty's feet, a gesture of respect and gratitude for the comfort she had given me. With a heart full of mixed emotions, I hurried back to my aunt's house.

It felt as if I had grown wings today, soaring high with an uncontainable joy. I found myself jumping on the sofa, my laughter echoing through the room, and dancing with an abandon I hadn't felt in years. There was no music, yet every color seemed more vivid, as if a rainbow had burst into life inside the house. I didn't want to stop; it was as if someone had tied tiny bells to my feet, their sweet tinkling filling my ears. Everywhere I turned, I could hear the enchanting melody of a flute, as if Krishna himself had come to play for me, and I was dancing like Radha, lost in the pure bliss of the moment.

I didn't know how to fall in love with someone, or if what I felt was love or something else entirely. All I knew was that I wanted to break free from all restrictions and be captured in this moment forever. The lines between right and wrong blurred, and I didn't care to distinguish them. The fear of losing this newfound happiness was the only thing that threatened to crush my wings, suppressing the joyful sound of my anklets and draining the vibrant colors from my life. It was a delicate balance between holding onto this bliss and the fear of it slipping away.

Love is a complex and beautiful emotion that doesn't adhere to strict rules or timelines. It's perfectly natural to feel happy when Bhaskar looks at you, and those feelings can be a sign of love or a deep affection. There's no specific age to fall in love; it can happen at any time and often catches us by surprise.

As for the mind and heart, it's a delicate balance. While the heart can guide us with its emotions and desires, the mind helps us navigate the practicalities and realities of life. It's important to listen to both, allowing your heart to feel and your mind to think, so you can make decisions that bring you happiness and fulfillment.

Ultimately, love is about finding joy and connection with someone, and it's okay to embrace those feelings without overanalyzing them. Trust yourself and your emotions, and let your journey unfold naturally.

The doorbell rang, and it felt as though all my desires would end with that single chime. With a heavy heart, I reluctantly got up and made my way to the door. As I opened it, I forced a smile and said, "Hi, Jiju," doing my best to conceal the sadness that lingered within me.

"You are not ready yet," Di exclaimed as she walked in, her eyes scanning the room. "And what is the state of the house? Did you drink again? Get ready quickly; it's time for the movie."

"Jiju, do you also get orders like this?" I asked my brother-in-law with a playful grin. I quickly tidied up the house and rushed to get ready, knowing another scolding was imminent if I delayed.

"Come on, I'm ready!" I announced, hurrying downstairs. "And you still haven't made your tea," I teased Di.

"Let's have some tea in the car," Di suggested, handing out tea cups to everyone.

"Jiju, don't you say anything? Ever since you came, you've only said hello," I remarked as we settled into the car.

"You're arguing a lot today. Sit quietly; we're getting late," Di replied, taking her seat.

"See, Di said it again. You're still quiet," I teased Jiju, enjoying the playful banter.

With laughter and light-hearted teasing, we finally reached the movie hall. Oh, I almost forgot to tell you—we went to see Stree 2.

During the interval, my brother-in-law and I stepped out to get some popcorn. With a playful grin, I asked, "Does it ever happen that someone falls in love with a ghost?"

For the first time, Jiju spoke up, and his words left me speechless. "Love definitely happens," he said thoughtfully. "Love does not happen by looking at caste, religion, right or wrong, age, looks, or whether the other person is alive or dead. Love is just love; it happens."

His profound words resonated deeply, silencing my playful banter and leaving me with much to ponder.

When the movie ended and we were heading home, my sister couldn't resist teasing me. "What happened? Did some headless ghost start following you that you've stopped talking? You were so chatty on the way here, what's changed now?"

Instead of answering Di's playful question, I turned the tables. "How did you both fall in love with each other?"

"You've asked a very good question," Di said, smiling. She turned to Jiju and added, "Give me the answer, I want to hear it too."

Jiju took a deep breath and began, "Your sister was my junior, and one day she came to our class with some accounts-related problem for Ganesh Sir." He paused and looked at Di, adding with a chuckle, "My Ganesh Sir." This was clearly an inside joke between them, and they both burst into laughter.

He continued, "So, while she was asking her question, her hair kept falling on her face. The way she kept tucking it behind her ears made my heart skip a beat each time. When she finally left the class, to tell you the truth, my heart stopped beating altogether. From that moment on, I couldn't stop thinking about her, and I came home."

"Came home? What do you mean?" I asked, utterly shocked.

Sarika Di, sitting in the front seat, turned around and said, "Hey fool, you've reached your home."

"Jiju, let's go home, I'm really enjoying your story," I insisted, turning to my sister and pleading with them both. After some convincing, they agreed.

We all headed straight to Di's room. I grabbed my favorite spot, the bean bag, and eagerly said, "Yes, start now."

Jiju continued, "When I didn't see her in college for a few days, I finally asked her friend why Sarika wasn't coming. That's when I found out her grandfather had passed away and today was his Tiye Baithak in the evening." He paused, looking at Di with a silent apology in his eyes.

Then he continued, "So I gathered my friends and went straight to her house, attending the Tiye Baithak just to see her. That night, I couldn't sleep at all. I decided that no matter what, I would propose to her the next day. Before everyone went to college, I took a rose and a beautiful card and went to Sarika." He paused, then got up and went to Sarika Di, kneeling down and taking her hand in his. "I love you, Sarika. I love you very much, not because you are beautiful, but because without you, my breath feels incomplete. Since the day I saw you, you have become the purpose of my life. You can refuse if you want."

Di interrupted him, looking at me with a smile. "Till now, whatever he has said is what everyone says, but what he said next made me say yes to him the very next day. Now listen."

Jiju continued, "If you want, you can refuse. I will never come back into your path, but it is also true that I will never be able to belong to anyone else."

His heartfelt confession left me in awe, understanding why Di had fallen for him. Their love story was truly special, filled with genuine emotion and deep connection.

Hearing this I stood up and started clapping and went and hugged them both and said "It was so much fun, so cute, so romantic."

It was time for Aunty and Uncle to come so Di said "Now you go or else mummy will complain"

I said, "It is 7 o'clock right now and both of them are not going to come before 8:30, so you still have time, and even if they come, I will tell them that I have called them and I want to talk to my brother-in-law."

"You go and make something cold for me and Jiju, go," I told Di and gestured for her to leave.

Di teased me and went away from there and brought a cold drink from the fridge kept in front.

"Brother-in-law, what were you saying there in the hall that one can fall in love with anyone and all", I told my brother-in-law and went and sat next to Didi.

Jiju smiled, clearly enjoying the moment. "Love is like a river," he began, "it flows naturally, carving its own path, sometimes gentle and sometimes fierce. It doesn't ask for permission; it just happens. When two people find each other, their hearts beat in sync, creating a rhythm that only they can hear."

"Rhythm?" I asked, intrigued by the concept.

"Yes," Jiju replied with a gentle smile. "Love is a feeling that does not believe in any boundaries; it only understands emotions. Love does not see who is in front of you because love is blind, and it only understands the rhythm. One falls in love with the one whose rhythm matches. It is not without reason that Shiri became Farhad's, that Heer became Ranjha's, that Juliet became Romeo's, and that Sarika became Anand's."

His words painted a beautiful picture of love as a harmonious dance, where two souls find their perfect rhythm together. It made me realize that love is about finding that unique connection, where hearts beat in sync and create a melody that only they can hear.

Di and I listened intently, captivated by his words. "Love is also about understanding and accepting each other," he continued. "It's about seeing the beauty in someone's flaws and standing by them through thick and thin. It's not always perfect, but it's real and it's worth fighting for."

I couldn't help but feel a sense of awe. "Wow, Jiju, you really are a guru," I said, grinning. "Tell us more!"

He chuckled, "Well, love is also about growth. It's about helping each other become the best versions of ourselves. It's a journey, not a destination. And sometimes, it's the little things that matter the most—the shared laughter, the silent support, the unspoken understanding."

As he spoke, I realized how profound and multifaceted love truly is. It was a beautiful lesson, one that I would carry with me for a long time.

Jiju's words were profound, resonating deeply with both Di and me. "Love is the respect that we give to our partner and hope that they give us the same respect in return. What made Heer smilingly sacrifice her life for Ranjha? It was the respect Ranjha gave to Heer, and that respect is immortal, an ideal for lovers like us," he explained.

"Jiju, how do we know that we are in love with someone?" I asked eagerly.

"We believe that we have fallen in love with this man or that woman, but the reality is that love makes its own way. It makes you meet the person who is made only for you, or you meet the woman who is made only for you. We don't find love; love finds us," he said, effortlessly clearing my doubt.

Di, sensing where my thoughts were headed, gave me an awkward look and asked Jiju, "And what about society? If the boy is from a different caste or not within our societal norms, what should we do? Society won't accept that girl or boy, right?"

"These differences of caste, religion, and age have been created by us as humans for our convenience. These are the hypocrisies of society that are hollowing out human emotions and preventing them from loving each other," he replied.

"And age, what if age is coming in the way?" Di asked.

"Why does a mother not stop loving her child until her death? Why does a father want to hug his child? Do they look at age? No, they only look at emotions. They only love. Today, if someone loses their leg in an accident, will their parents abandon them? No, that is true love, real affection," Jiju explained.

His words left us both in deep thought, understanding that love transcends societal boundaries and norms, focusing purely on the emotions and connections between people.

"If we feel such love for someone, then never let them go," Jiju said with conviction.

"And if love is one-sided?" Di asked, her voice tinged with curiosity.

Jiju took a deep breath and replied, "Didn't Radha know that she wouldn't be able to be Krishna's in that life? Didn't Krishna know that he wouldn't be able to be Meera's? Yet, today we learn how to love from Radha, Meera, and Krishna. Their love became immortal because of the respect they had for each other's emotions, decisions, and pain. Love does not mean possessing or achieving someone; love is just love, it happens."

His words resonated deeply, highlighting that true love transcends the need for reciprocation. It's about honoring and cherishing the feelings we hold, even if they aren't returned in the way we hope. Love, in its purest form, is about respect and understanding, and that's what makes it timeless and beautiful.

Jiju paused, his hand on the doorknob, and turned back to face us. He took a moment to gather his thoughts before responding to Di's unexpected question.

"If the man is of the age of the girl's father, then what should she do?" he repeated thoughtfully.

"He should at least get a chance. If the love is true, it will carve its own path. Just don't hinder it. Let it flow, for love is as pure as the Ganga. Every day, the sins of the world are washed away in its waters, yet the Ganga remains untainted. This is the essence of true love. The mind may attempt to tarnish it, but if love flows from the heart, no matter how much the mind tries, the heart will always prevail."

"Age is just a number, but it's important to consider the dynamics of the relationship. If both individuals share a deep connection, mutual respect, and genuine love, then age should not be a barrier. However, it's also crucial to think about the practical aspects and societal perceptions. The most important thing is that both people are happy and comfortable with their relationship. Love should bring joy and fulfillment, not confusion or distress."

He looked at Di and then at me, his eyes filled with sincerity. "Ultimately, it's about what feels right for both people involved. Love is about understanding, respect, and mutual happiness. If those elements are present, then age differences can be navigated with care and consideration."

With that, he gave us a reassuring smile, hugged Di once more, and waved goodbye to me before heading out. Di and I sat in silence for a moment, absorbing his words and the wisdom they carried.

In that moment, Jiju became a hero in our eyes. Didi glanced at me, and I returned her gaze. Without a word, we both went to bed and lay there in silence, each lost in our own thoughts. Just as I was about to ask Didi why she had posed that question to Jiju, she turned to me and asked, "Did you meet Bhaskar today?"

"Didi, I just went to return Divyasha's diary," I replied, my voice tinged with fear.

"There isn't much time left before my marriage. You have only seven days. After that, I'll be moving to Anand's house, and Aunty will take you back to Delhi with her. How will you get to know Bhaskar uncle—I mean, Bhaskar—well in such a short time?" When Didi said this, I felt a wave of relief wash over me.

"Didi, Didi!"

"Yes, speak, I am listening," Sarika Di responded, still in shock. She hadn't realized that Divyasha was standing behind her. She had been talking to me with her head bowed, thinking it was me who had called her. I gently placed my hand on her shoulder. When she looked up at me, I gestured towards her, indicating that I wasn't the one calling her. "Look behind," I signaled.

When Sarika Di turned around, she saw Divyasha standing there, calling her.

"When did you come?" Sarika Di asked, clearly shocked. She worried that Divyasha might have overheard everything.

"Just now," she replied, moving closer to Di and hugging her tightly. "Thank you, Di. If you hadn't gotten married, Niharika Di would never have come into our lives. And if she hadn't come into our lives, everything that has happened wouldn't have happened."

"What happened?" Sarika Di asked, her curiosity piqued.

"Have you not told Di yet, Niharika Di?" Divyasha asked, turning her gaze towards me.

"I haven't had the time yet; Jiju had come over," I said, making an excuse to avoid the topic.

"It doesn't matter, I'll tell you. A miracle has happened, Didi. A scolding from Niharika Di has brought a lot of change in Papa," Divyasha said, moving to stand beside me.

Placing her hand on my shoulder, she said, "Today, Bhaskar asked me to go for a walk with him. He even put his cigarette packet away in the drawer of his room right in front of me. That's why I came to ask if you, Niharika Di, would join us for the walk."

"I will also come," said Sarika Di, quickly putting on her shoes and getting ready.

When the three of us were ready and came downstairs, we saw Bhaskar already walking in the park. We joined him, and as we started walking together, Bhaskar greeted us with a cheerful "hi" to both Sarika Di and me.

Sarika Di looked like she might faint after hearing Bhaskar's greeting. After three rounds of the park, Divyasha and Sarika sat down on a bench, but my excitement was at its peak. It was a new love affair, and I couldn't help but keep walking step by step with Bhaskar.

Walking with Bhaskar was exhilarating. My heart was racing with excitement, and every step felt like a new adventure. It was a mix of nervousness and joy, knowing that this was the beginning of something special. The conversation flowed effortlessly, and I couldn't help but feel a strong connection forming between us.

Yes, you heard it right. After listening to my brother-in-law's words, all my troubles seemed to vanish like mist in the morning sun. I felt a newfound clarity and courage. No longer would I be afraid to tell the whole world that I have fallen deeply, irrevocably in love with Bhaskar Sharma. His age and the years that separate us mean nothing to me now. What matters is the love that fills my heart, pure and unwavering.

Right now, I may not have the words to fully express the depth of my feelings to him, but I know that day will come. A day when I will stand tall and proclaim to the entire world, "Bhaskar Sharma, I love you! I love you with all my heart and soul, and nothing else matters." The thought of that moment fills me with a thrilling anticipation, a promise of a love that is as boundless as the sky.

"Di, you know how eagerly I have waited for this day, to see my father happy and full of life," Divyasha said to Sarika Di, her voice filled with emotion.

Sarika Di's eyes softened as she listened, understanding the depth of Divyasha's feelings. It was a moment of shared relief and joy, knowing that her father's transformation was a testament to the power of love and support.

Divyasha paused, taking a deep breath before continuing. "You know, Didi, a boy proposed to me in school. He was handsome and probably liked me a lot. I liked him too, but I turned him down because I was terrified. I was scared that if I had even 0.1% of my mother's genes, I would ruin his life just like she ruined my father's."

Sarika Di listened intently, her expression softening with understanding and compassion. "Oh, Divyasha," she said gently, "you are not defined by your mother's mistakes. You are your own person, capable of making your own choices and creating your own path. Don't let fear hold you back from experiencing love and happiness."

Both of them watched us, laughing and walking together, but Bhaskar and I were lost in our own world. Our steps were in perfect harmony, neither faltering. In my mind, I wished that our entire lives could pass by just like this—walking side by side, supporting each other through every stumble and worry. If he ever stopped or felt troubled, I would be there to care for him. And if I ever needed to pause or felt anxious, he would be there to support me. I hoped our journey would continue like this, filled with laughter and joy.

Sarika Di had no words to respond to Divyasha's heartfelt confession, so she simply listened. Then, Divyasha said something that brought tears to Sarika Di's eyes. She hugged Divyasha tightly "I wish my mother had been like Niharika Di. Then we all would have lived together so happily."

CHAPTER FOUR

First Date

A new morning, a fresh beginning! With this mantra echoing in my mind, I sprang out of bed at the crack of dawn. Yesterday, while strolling with Bhaskar, we had made an exciting plan. Today, we would venture to a serene, distant spot for our morning walk and bask in the breathtaking beauty of Ajmer's valleys.

Sarika Di was still peacefully asleep, and I didn't have the heart to wake her. So, I quickly freshened up, slipped into my jogging suit, and headed straight to Bhaskar's house. When I rang the bell, Bhaskar promptly opened the gate with a cheerful "Let's go!" and we set off on our walk together.

We had barely taken two steps when the sea of questions in my restless mind overflowed. I couldn't hold back any longer and started talking to Bhaskar. To kick off the conversation, I confessed, "I couldn't sleep the whole night."

"Why?" Bhaskar asked curiosity evident in his voice.

I felt a strong urge to confess that I lost sleep because of my feelings for him, but I held back and said, "I don't know, maybe I lost sleep waiting to see the valleys." Wow, what an excuse, Niharika! You couldn't have come up with anything better? I thought to myself, feeling a bit embarrassed. I fell silent and continued walking straight ahead.

"Hmm, Ajmer looks so beautiful in the rainy season," Bhaskar mused. Then, pointing towards the hill above, he added, "A waterfall flows from here. When I was young, I used to come here with my friends."

"Let's go now," I insisted, eager to explore. Bhaskar nodded, and with a smile, we began our ascent towards the waterfall.

"How will I be able to climb so high at this age?" Bhaskar said, gazing up at the valleys with a hint of doubt in his eyes.

But I am a stubborn person, and I just followed him up the hill. For a moment, I worried that this might be the first and last time we do this, and that he might start hating me. He kept refusing and was reluctant to go, so I took his hand and led him forward. He began walking with me, holding my hand like a small child. When we reached the hill, I understood why he had been hesitant. The hill was incredibly high, almost touching the sky. But having already committed, I started climbing, and he followed me.

"You are very stubborn," Bhaskar said, smiling warmly.

"Not much, just a little," I replied with a smile.

If you think I was about to fall and Bhaskar would catch me like in a Hindi movie, let me clarify that nothing of the sort happened. But yes, something did occur that shattered not just my mind but also my soul. We both stopped at a point. Bhaskar still had the stamina to climb higher, but my bones were giving up. One more step, and I would have needed an ambulance.

"I've seen the waterfall; I don't need to see it again. Let's sit here and head back home tomorrow," I declared, bursting into laughter.

Bhaskar laughed too and sat down beside me. As I caught my breath, he said, "Thank you, Niharika. It's been a long time since I laughed like this. Thank you for reminding me of my responsibilities. Divyasha's life is getting ruined because of me. I am the culprit. Ayesha was right, and I was wrong."

I held his hand and said, "If you were wrong and she was right, then today, instead of you, she would be sitting on this hill and crying."

"But I turned out to be weak, and she still has her courage," he said, trying to suppress the pain inside.

"Can you tell me your story from the beginning? I really want to know," I said to him, my curiosity piqued.

"In those days, I had a lot of fun with my friends in Ajmer. I was young and quite popular among the girls. I was confident and smart, and my friends often came to me to solve their problems. I was so positive about life that my friends sometimes got jealous and asked how I stayed so chill. I always credited my father for my positivity. I had set small goals for myself, knowing exactly what to do, where to do it, and how much to achieve. The biggest goal of my life was to serve my parents. I never wanted to leave them, which is why I decided to stay in Ajmer."

"So what happened that made you leave Ajmer and go to Delhi?" I asked, genuinely curious.

Bhaskar bowed his head and said, "Then she came into my life and turned all my dreams upside down. First, she argued with me and pushed me to leave Ajmer, saying there was no growth here and I wouldn't achieve anything. I started to see how much she cared about my future, so I went to Delhi and started working. Being smart and educated, I quickly found a job. Yes, I was from a small town and lacked certain manners, but I gradually learned. After two years of working in Delhi, I was settled, and her parents were also ready, so we got married soon."

"Before marriage, did you ever feel that she was controlling you? Or did you never try to understand what was on her mind?" I asked, genuinely curious.

"Before marriage, she never said anything that would hurt my feelings. In fact, sometimes I felt like I was becoming too bossy. She made me feel guilty about it, and I felt the same way. So, I gradually stopped saying anything that might make her feel I was being bossy," Bhaskar explained.

"How did the distance grow between you two?" I asked, wanting to understand more.

"From the very first night after our marriage, distance started to grow between us," he said, his voice tinged with sadness.

Bhaskar looked at me and said, "You're a medical student, so I can tell you if you permit."

I didn't say anything; I just nodded my head to indicate yes.

Then he started telling his story. "Our relationship was three years old, but we were a bit traditional compared to today's generation. We decided to wait until marriage for any physical contact. But whenever I touched her after marriage, she made me feel like I was doing something wrong." He fell silent after saying this, clenching his fist in frustration.

When I noticed this, I gently caressed his fist with my hand. He took a deep breath, and I asked softly, "What happened next?"

"Why? Why would any woman do this? She loved you too, right?" I asked, trying to understand.

He started speaking again, "I slowly began to fear touching her. She started making new excuses, sometimes showing me videos about vaginismus on the internet. Other times, she would accuse her brother Anshuman, saying he had touched her inappropriately during childhood, which made her uncomfortable with intimacy. A strange fear began to grow inside me. I even stopped myself from accidentally touching her. I started to believe she had suffered a lot, and I felt I had to suppress my own feelings for her sake. I thought I needed to make this sacrifice for my love."

He was fuming in anger, his face flushed a deep crimson, but I knew intervening now would only fan the flames. His breath came in ragged gasps as he began to speak, his voice trembling with a mix of frustration and sorrow.

"But I was young," he said, his eyes glistening with unshed tears, "and it was impossible for me to control myself. I took her to all the best doctors in Delhi, hoping for a miracle. Each one told me the same thing: she doesn't want this, she has no disease. But she had me convinced otherwise. With a cunning blend of love and anger, she silenced me every time, manipulating my emotions with a deftness that left me powerless. This torment went on for two whole years."

His voice was laden with such profound despair, it was as if someone had hurled a stone from a towering cliff, and it was plummeting with a hopelessness that nothing and no one could halt.

"Now, I had completely lost hope," he continued, his tone a haunting echo of his shattered dreams. "I had killed this desire; buried it deep within my heart. I resolved that I would never look at her in that way again."

He took a deep breath, trying to steady himself before continuing. "And I had told her about this too," he said, his voice now a whisper of its former intensity. "Then, suddenly, one day she provoked me, and everything seemed to resolve itself without any issue. I was bewildered by how it happened and began to see myself as a criminal. I felt like a rapist, believing I had forced myself upon her. The guilt was overwhelming, and from that day on, I became her slave. Whenever she said 'get up,' I would get up; whenever she said 'sit,' I would sit. Whatever she commanded, I obeyed without question. I carried the weight of this guilt for nearly a year, and then what happened next completely devastated me."

I wiped my eyes, trying to steady my voice as I asked Bhaskar, "So, did she really have Vaginismus?"

Bhaskar took a deep breath, his eyes reflecting a mixture of sadness and resignation. "She was doing all this knowingly," he began, his voice steady but tinged with sorrow. "She didn't want to have a child. She had dreams of securing a good job and making something of herself. That's why she secretly took contraceptive pills every day."

I screamed, my voice echoing with disbelief, "What? Really? You mean nothing was happening between you two, you weren't even having sex, and she was still taking medicines to prevent pregnancy?"

"Yes," he replied, his voice heavy with the weight of betrayal. "And when I found out and confronted her in anger, she turned it all back on me and my mother. She called me an uneducated person, a small-town guy with a narrow mindset. She made me feel that the success I've achieved in my job was solely because of her, implying that without her, I'd be stuck in some small job in Ajmer.

I started to believe her, thinking maybe she was right. I forgot about the medicine and convinced myself that she truly loved me."

"But she was wrong," I said, my voice filled with frustration. "Why didn't you take any steps at that time?"

He gave a sheepish smile, a hint of sadness in his eyes. "I started living with this guilt every day," he said softly. "It became a constant in my life. Every time I tried to touch her, she made me feel like I was doing something wrong. And finally, one day..."

He fell into deep thought, his voice softening as he continued. "I mustered up the courage and told her that whatever we do should be mutual, as it is for any husband and wife. If you feel that the way I touch you is wrong, please tell me openly what you like, and I will be mindful of it from now on. She then told me that she prefers to be intimate during the day, not at night, and that I only approached her at night. I explained that we both work during the day, so we only have time at night, but if she prefers it during the day, we could make time on Sundays."

He stopped speaking, his silence heavy with unspoken pain. It was as if his words had reached their limit, but the cruelty he endured from that woman had not.

I leaned in closer, my curiosity piqued. "What happened next?" I asked, my voice barely above a whisper.

He composed himself, taking a deep breath before continuing. "Then every Sunday, she started planning outings and wouldn't return home until night. She began to insult me over this issue, making me feel inadequate. Over these four years, I started to believe that maybe something was lacking in me."

"I decorated the room for her, hoping she would appreciate it," he said, his voice tinged with a mix of hope and resignation. "I tried to change myself for her. I used to enjoy wearing shorts when I was relaxing at home, but for her, I started wearing pajamas even when I was just sitting around."

"After doing all this, she would have no excuse left. What happened next?" I asked, my curiosity growing.

"When she ran out of other excuses, she started attacking me directly," he said, his voice filled with a mix of frustration and sadness. "She'd say things like, 'You smell of sweat,' or 'You have too much hair on your body.' Gradually, I began to feel disgusted with my own body. I started using new soaps every day and sprayed perfume all over the house, trying to mask any scent. But despite all my efforts, she kept insisting that I never loved her, that I married her only for sex. Whenever I tried to touch her playfully, she would call me a pervert."

He fell silent, the weight of his words hanging heavily in the air.

"So you didn't get angry after hearing all this?" I asked, my voice filled with disbelief.

"When she said those things, I didn't get angry at her," he continued, his voice filled with resignation. "Instead, I believed her. I thought she was right and I was wrong, so I stopped trying. It wasn't that I felt bad because she couldn't or didn't want to do those things; I felt bad because she made me feel responsible for it. If she had just told me the truth once, I would have accepted it and lived my life accordingly. But she always blamed me, making me feel like a rapist every single time."

I listened quietly to Bhaskar, holding back my tears. I knew that if I tried to speak, they would start flowing uncontrollably. But then a thought struck me, and I asked, "Then Divyasha?"

"Yes, she is our daughter, but..." Bhaskar's voice trailed off, leaving the sentence hanging in the air, heavy with unspoken words.

"But, but what, Bhaskar? Tell me, I want to know," I urged him, my voice trembling with anticipation.

"That was a plan," he said, his voice filled with a mix of bitterness and sorrow. "By then, I was so broken that I had stopped touching her and even looking at her. She started thinking I was no longer under her control, but that wasn't true—I was still in her grip. So, she provoked me for sex, knowing we didn't have condoms. She didn't stop me until I lost control, and when it was over, she blamed me so harshly that I felt like committing suicide. My life was consumed by fear."

"Afraid, why?" I asked, my voice barely a whisper, filled with concern and curiosity.

"Ever since Ayesha came into my life, I've lived in constant fear," Bhaskar said, his voice trembling. "Once, when no one was home, I wanted to listen to songs and have fun all night, but I felt too scared to do anything openly. It was as if any action I took would be wrong, and Ayesha would scold me. Gradually, I became so consumed by that fear that it felt like I had never experienced any other aspect of life. My mind was dominated by one thing: fear. Fear that Ayesha might get angry at something I said, because if she did, she would repeat the same accusations."

As he spoke, Bhaskar began to tremble, the weight of his emotions visibly overwhelming him.

I held his hand gently, trying to offer some comfort. "What did she say?" I asked softly, my voice filled with concern.

"You are of no use," Bhaskar said, his eyes wide open, filled with a haunting emptiness. Tears welled up but seemed to dry before they could fall. He spoke, his voice trembling with fear and despair.

He looked at me, perhaps drawing some strength from my presence, and continued, "Then she started breaking household items, screaming that I was the biggest blot on her life. She said I was worth nothing, that I had never done anything good and never would. She claimed that everyone in my family thought I was useless, that I was helpless and didn't know anything. She said everything got spoiled just by being around me, that I was a negative person."

As he spoke, tears began to stream down his face, his body shaking with sobs. "She used to stop me from doing any work, always saying that I didn't know anything. Whenever I mustered the courage to do something, she would find so many flaws that I became terrified of trying again. I started to believe her words—that I was truly useless."

"Even after becoming a mother, doesn't she understand that she's doing wrong?" I asked, my voice filled with a mix of disbelief and concern.

It seemed I had touched a raw nerve. As soon as I mentioned Divyasha, Bhaskar's demeanor changed drastically. He lost his temper, his teeth grinding in pain, and his body began to tremble, his fists clenched tightly.

With a gentle touch on his shoulder, I leaned in closer, my voice a soothing whisper amidst the storm of his emotions. "Bhaskar," I began, my words tender and inviting, "please, pour out all your pain. Let it flow like a river unburdened by judgment. I am here, not to judge, but to listen, to understand. Share your heart with me."

His eyes, once clouded with the weight of unspoken sorrows, began to glisten with the promise of release. The room seemed to hold its breath, waiting for the dam to break, for the flood of his anguish to finally find its voice.

Bhaskar's voice trembled as he let his anger flow, each word a heavy stone dropping into the silence between us. "Once, when Divyasha was small," he began, his eyes distant, lost in the painful memory, "I took her to bathe. Her hair got tangled, and in her frustration, she humiliated me so deeply that from that day on, I never dared to collect any sweet memories of my cute little girl's childhood."

His confession hung in the air, raw and unfiltered. The room seemed to shrink around us, the weight of his sorrow pressing in. I could see the years of hurt etched into his face, the regret of lost moments with his daughter. It was a wound that had festered, hidden beneath layers of silence and unspoken pain.

Bhaskar shook his head slowly, the weight of his silence evident in his downcast eyes. "No," he murmured, his voice barely above a whisper. "I never told anyone. I felt... ashamed, I suppose. Ashamed that I couldn't handle such a simple thing, that my own daughter could make me feel so small."

He paused, taking a deep breath as if trying to steady himself. "I thought it was my burden to bear alone. I didn't want to seem weak or incapable. So, I kept it all inside, letting it eat away at me bit by bit."

The room seemed to grow quieter, the air thick with the unspoken pain that had been locked away for so long. I could see the struggle in his eyes, the battle between the desire to unburden himself and the fear of being judged. "But now," he continued, his voice gaining a hint of strength, "maybe it's time to let it out. Maybe it's time to heal."

Bhaskar's voice grew more intense, the bitterness of his experiences seeping into every word. "She left no stone unturned to prove me a zero in the eyes of everybody," he said, his eyes flashing with a mix of anger and sorrow. "My parents, my siblings, my colleagues at work—wherever I tried to reclaim a piece of my old self, she would come and humiliate me for some reason or another."

He paused, his hands clenching into fists as he relived the countless moments of degradation. "It was like she had a mission to break me down, to ensure I never felt worthy or capable. Every time I tried to stand up, she was there to knock me down again."

The pain in his voice was palpable, a testament to the years of emotional turmoil he had endured. I could see the toll it had taken on him, the way it had eroded his confidence and self-worth. "But Bhaskar," I said gently, "you are not alone in this. You don't have to carry this burden by yourself anymore. It's time to let go of the past and start healing. You deserve to find peace and happiness again."

As Bhaskar's words trailed off, his composure shattered. He began to cry loudly, the sound raw and heart-wrenching. His hands, trembling with the weight of his emotions, fumbled in his pocket for a pack of cigarettes. Each movement was a desperate attempt to find some semblance of control amidst the chaos of his feelings.

I reached out, gently placing my hand over his to still the shaking. "Bhaskar," I said softly, "it's okay to feel this way. It's okay to let it all out. You don't have to hide behind anything anymore."

His sobs filled the atmosphere, a cathartic release of years of pent-up pain. I stayed by his side, offering silent support, knowing that sometimes, the most powerful thing you can do for someone is simply to be there, to let them know they are not alone in their suffering.

I caught his trembling hand and pressed it against my chest, feeling the rapid beat of my heart beneath his fingers. Pulling him into a tight embrace, I whispered fervently, "Now everything is over, Bhaskar. I am here in your life now. Nothing like this will happen again. I will give you all the happiness that you have lost till date."

But his pain was a deep, unyielding chasm, so vast that my words seemed to vanish into it. He continued to cry, his body shaking with the force of his sobs, unable to feel my touch or hear my voice. It was as if he was trapped in a storm of his own making, unreachable despite my best efforts.

I held him tighter, hoping that my presence alone could offer some comfort, some small measure of solace in his darkest hour. And though he couldn't yet feel it, I vowed silently to stand by him, to help him find his way back to the light.

I began to gently caress his back, my touch a silent promise of support. Gradually, his sobs softened, and he started to calm down. After a while, he reached out and caressed my head, his touch so pure, so gentle, so full of intimacy. "Now we should go home," he said softly.

In that moment, I was struck by the depth of his kindness. Here was a man, broken and hurting, yet capable of such tenderness. I couldn't help but wonder how much love and care he must have shown to his wife, the woman he loved so deeply. It was a poignant reminder of the complexity of human emotions, and the strength it takes to remain gentle in the face of so much pain.

I nodded in agreement, and together, hand in hand, we began our descent from the mountain. The silence between us was profound, filled with the unspoken words and shared understanding. We walked for some distance, the only sounds being the crunch of gravel underfoot and the whisper of the wind.

He remained silent, perhaps because he had already poured out so much of his heart. As for me, I held my tongue, knowing that if I spoke, my words would betray the depth of my feelings for him. In that quiet moment, I realized how much I cared for him, how deeply his pain had touched me.

The journey down the mountain was a silent testament to our bond, a promise of support and understanding. And though words were left unspoken, the connection between us grew stronger with each step we took together.

I looked at him, the weight of the moment still heavy in the air. "Can you give me a cigarette?" I asked softly, my voice barely breaking the silence.

He paused, his eyes meeting mine with a mixture of surprise and understanding. Without a word, he reached into his pocket and handed me a cigarette. As I took it from him, our fingers brushed, and for a brief moment, the connection between us felt even more tangible.

We stood there, side by side, the unspoken bond between us growing stronger with each passing second. The cigarette was just a small gesture, but it symbolized so much more—a shared moment of vulnerability, a step towards healing, and the beginning of a deeper understanding between us.

Bhaskar, with a silent resolve, reached into his pocket and retrieved a crumpled packet of cigarettes. Without uttering a word, he offered me one, his eyes meeting mine with a knowing look. He placed another between his own lips, the unspoken camaraderie hanging in the air. With a flick of his lighter, he ignited the tip of my cigarette first, the flame dancing briefly before moving to his own. The first drag was a shared moment of quiet understanding, the smoke curling upwards in the dim light.

And then he started walking. His pace quickened, and I could sense the simmering anger in his stride. He moved two steps ahead, leaving me trailing behind. The gap widened to four steps, and I felt the distance growing not just physically but emotionally.

"Bhaskar," I called out, my voice cutting through the tension. He halted, turning slightly. "Can we sit here for a while? Let's finish our cigarettes and then leave."

"You are not angry with me, are you?" I asked, my voice tinged with guilt. I knew that our conversation had dredged up painful memories for him, and the weight of it hung heavy between us. I felt a pang of regret, wishing I could take back the words that had caused him to remember all those things again.

"Why would I be angry with you?" he said, a calm smile spreading across his face. His demeanor was unexpectedly serene, and it eased some of the tension I felt. The warmth in his eyes reassured me, and for a moment, the weight of our earlier conversation seemed to lift.

"Because I made you remember all of this again," I told him, my voice barely above a whisper. The guilt gnawed at me, and I couldn't shake the feeling that I had reopened old wounds.

Bhaskar's smile didn't waver. "Memories are tricky," he said softly, taking a slow drag from his cigarette. "But they don't control us. We do."

He took a long drag from his cigarette, the ember glowing brightly in the dim light. As he exhaled, the smoke curled around us, creating a momentary veil. "I had never forgotten all this," he began, his voice steady but reflective. "In fact, I feel good after sharing it with you. Until now, I haven't been able to tell anyone so openly."

He paused, his eyes meeting mine with a mixture of gratitude and relief. "Actually, I should thank you for listening to me for so long and tolerating my nonsense.

Since the day I got married, my wife has never really talked to me. She would always do the talking, and I would just listen silently. If I ever went out or tried to talk to someone, she would jump into every conversation and push me aside."

His words hung in the air, heavy with the weight of unspoken emotions. I could see the years of silence and suppression etched into his expression, and I felt a deep sense of empathy for him.

I cursed that woman silently in my mind, feeling a surge of anger on Bhaskar's behalf. Then, turning to him, I said, "Whatever happened is done. Let's make a new beginning."

With that, I sprang to my feet and started running, the cool night air filling my lungs. Bhaskar watched me for a moment, then a smile broke across his face. He stubbed out his cigarette and joined me, our laughter echoing in the stillness as we ran into the unknown, ready to embrace whatever came next.

Then I looked back at Bhaskar and shouted, "Catch me!" My voice rang out, playful and challenging.

For a moment, he stood there, surprised by my sudden burst of energy. Then, with a grin spreading across his face, he took off after me. The morning air was filled with our laughter as we raced through the empty streets, leaving behind the weight of old memories and embracing the promise of new beginnings.

I wanted Bhaskar to come running and take me in his arms, but I knew that hurt lover wasn't going to melt so easily. "Niharika," I whispered to myself, a reminder to stay strong. With renewed determination, I started running again, my feet pounding against the pavement. The morning was alive with possibilities, and I was ready to chase them all.

After running for some distance, I stopped, breathless and exhilarated. Bhaskar was right behind me, his footsteps slowing as he approached. It wasn't that he couldn't overtake me; he was running behind me intentionally, like a parent indulging a child's game. His eyes sparkled with a mix of amusement and affection, and in that moment, I realized he was letting me lead for my own happiness.

"Okay, I want to ask you something," I said, stopping to catch my breath. Bhaskar came to a halt beside me, his expression curious and attentive.

"What is it?" he asked, his voice gentle, as if ready to listen to whatever was on my mind.

"You just said that you felt good after telling me your story, so can we go to a cafe to have coffee today?" I asked, my breath coming in short gasps. "I like your company, and it will also lighten your mood. Tell me, what do you say? Look, such a beautiful girl is asking you to go for coffee at this age, so please don't refuse."

I bent down, hands on my knees, trying to catch my breath. Running wasn't exactly my forte, and the exertion was catching up to me. Bhaskar chuckled softly, his eyes twinkling with amusement.

"I am afraid to go out to a crowded place, please let us have coffee at home only," he said, his voice tinged with a hint of vulnerability.

"No, we will go outside, please, otherwise I will cry," I said, adding a touch of playful drama to my voice. I could see Bhaskar's resolve wavering, a smile tugging at the corners of his mouth.

"Alright, alright," he conceded, shaking his head with a chuckle. "How can I say no to that?"

And we both went to our respective homes. When I arrived, I recounted everything to Sarika Di, every word and every emotion. As I spoke, she started crying profusely, her tears mirroring my own. I tried to calm her down, but the problem was that my own tears were falling just as freely. We hugged each other tightly, sharing the weight of the moment.

Through her sobs, Sarika Di wiped my tears and asked, "What will you do now?"

"I am taking him on a coffee date this evening. I'm thinking of telling him my feelings there," I told Di, my voice trembling with a mix of excitement and nerves.

"This will happen very quickly. Give him some more time, and you yourself should also walk a little slowly," Didi said to me, her voice gentle but firm.

"Time is the only thing that matters, Didi. There isn't much time left before your wedding. In a few days, guests will start arriving, and Mom and Dad will also come. When will I get a chance to tell him what's in my heart?" I said, my voice filled with urgency.

"You are right, but it will be too early," Didi explained, her tone firm yet caring. "Not today. Just have coffee today and come back. First, understand him completely. What will you do if he turns out to be wrong?"

Her words made sense, and I could see the wisdom in her advice. "Alright, Didi," I said, nodding slowly. "I'll take it slow and just enjoy the coffee today."

She smiled, relieved. "That's my girl. Take your time and let things unfold naturally."

Di got up and brought out a lovely suit from her wardrobe, her eyes sparkling with a mix of nostalgia and hope. "Wear this today," she said, handing it to me. "This is my lucky suit. I wore it when Anand proposed to me. I hope it proves lucky for you too."

I took the suit, feeling the soft fabric between my fingers. "Thank you, Didi," I said, touched by her gesture. "I'll wear it and hope for the best."

She smiled warmly. "Good luck. Just be yourself, and everything will fall into place."

"Ok Didi, now I am going to sleep for a while. I ran around a lot because of love today," I said with a smile, pulling the bed sheet over myself and switching off the lights. But as I lay there in the darkness, it became clear that this damned love had sworn to steal my sleep. My mind raced with thoughts of Bhaskar, the upcoming coffee date, and the possibilities that lay ahead. Despite my exhaustion, sleep remained elusive, replaced by a whirlwind of emotions and anticipation.

"Yes, go to sleep but don't go back to Bhaskar in your dreams," Didi teased, her laughter trailing behind her as she went downstairs.

I smiled to myself, pulling the bed sheet tighter around me. Despite her teasing, I knew she was right. My mind was already drifting back to thoughts of Bhaskar, and I couldn't help but wonder what the evening would bring. As I lay there, the excitement and anticipation kept me awake, my heart racing with the possibilities of what was to come.

After a while, Di came back upstairs. Seeing me tossing and turning, she came close and whispered in my ear, "Bhaskar's worshipper, go to sleep."

I couldn't help but laugh softly, her teasing breaking through my restless thoughts. "Alright, alright," I murmured, trying to settle down. Her presence was comforting, and I felt a bit more at ease. Maybe, just maybe, I could finally get some sleep.

Before I could say anything more, Divyasha came in, holding a steaming bowl of pasta. "I made this especially for you," she said with a smile, remembering our earlier conversation where I had mentioned my love for pasta.

The aroma was irresistible, and I felt a wave of gratitude. "Thank you, Divyasha," I said, sitting up and taking the bowl from her. "This is exactly what I needed."

She laughed softly. "Enjoy it, and try to get some rest. You have a big evening ahead."

As I took my first bite, the comforting taste of the pasta made me feel a little more grounded, ready to face whatever the evening would bring.

"How did you get to know about the evening plans?" I asked Divyasha, curiosity piqued.

She smiled and replied, "Bhaskar is my father, Didi. He told me about your coffee plans this evening."

I was taken aback for a moment, processing the unexpected revelation. "Oh, I see," I said, a smile spreading across my face. "Well, I hope he didn't give away too much."

Divyasha laughed. "Don't worry, he just mentioned the coffee. Enjoy your evening, Didi."

"Come, Divyasha, we were just talking about you," Sarika Didi said, her eyes twinkling with mischief as she teased me.

"You were talking about Bhaskar, not me, right, Niharika Di?" Divyasha said, sitting down next to me with a playful grin.

Di and I both fell silent, the weight of our thoughts hanging in the air. To break the tension, I quickly said, "Let me taste the pasta, quickly."

I took a generous forkful and savored the rich, comforting flavors. "Mmm, this is delicious, Divyasha!

You really outdid yourself."

Divyasha beamed with pride. "I'm glad you like it, Niharika Di. Enjoy every bite!"

The mood lightened, and we all shared a moment of warmth and laughter, the earlier heaviness lifting as we focused on the simple joy of good food and good company.

I didn't like hearing the word "didi" from her repeatedly, so I interrupted and said, "Please don't call me didi. I'm not older than you. Just like you call your father by his name, you should also call me by my name."

Divyasha looked a bit surprised but then smiled warmly. "Alright, Niharika," she said, emphasizing my name. "I'll remember that."

As I savored the pasta, an idea struck me. Why not find out Bhaskar's likes and dislikes from Divyasha? It would make it so much easier to impress him.

"Hey, Divyasha," I said, trying to sound casual. "Since we're talking about Bhaskar, can you tell me a bit more about his likes and dislikes? It would really help me get to know him better."

Divyasha smiled knowingly. "Sure, Niharika. What do you want to know?"

"Niharika, ever since I have been watching him, I have never seen him do anything of his own volition. It was always my mother who dictated every aspect of his life—what he would wear, what he would eat, when he would take a bath, and even when he would sleep. From the moment he opened his eyes in the morning to the second he closed them at night, he followed her commands without question. One day, in a fit of frustration, I scolded him, demanding to know why he never stood up to her. He just looked at me with those weary eyes, sighed deeply, and walked away in silence," Divyasha recounted, her voice tinged with a mix of sadness and exasperation.

Sarika Di, with a mix of curiosity and concern in her voice, asked Divyasha, "When all this was happening and you were aware of everything, why didn't you quickly escape from that woman's clutches?"

"Sister, I had no idea," Divyasha began, her voice trembling with a mix of regret and realization. "I myself misunderstood Bhaskar. I thought that Bhaskar was useless, but..." Her words trailed off, leaving an unspoken truth hanging in the air, her eyes reflecting a deep sorrow.

I couldn't contain my curiosity and asked Divyasha, "But, when did you find out that he is a victim of narcissistic abuse?"

She extended her hand towards Sarika Di, who gently took it in hers. With a timid voice, Divyasha said, "First of all, both of you please forgive me. I overheard everything you said the day Jiju came. I know that Niharika has started loving Bhaskar. I was standing on the stairs when Jiju left."

Before we could say anything, she quickly added, "But it's okay. I understand. And I haven't told anyone. This will always remain our secret. I promise."

Sarika Di, with the authority of an elder sister, asked firmly, "So now that you know everything, tell me clearly—do you support Niharika, or are you against this relationship?"

She came to me and hugged me tightly, whispering, "I like the new mummy, but what will we do about the old mummy?"

I was so overwhelmed with happiness that I didn't know what to do. Nervousness, love, joy, and a whirlwind of other emotions flooded my mind all at once. I grabbed the hands of Divyasha and Sarika Di, and we started jumping and dancing around, caught up in the moment. Then, I pulled them both into a tight hug, feeling the warmth of their support and love.

"Stop it, you're not married to Bhaskar yet! That poor guy doesn't even know what his daughter and neighbor are planning together," Sarika Di said, trying to calm me down. Turning to Divyasha, she added, "And you, don't get too happy just yet. She can become your mother, but she isn't your mother right now."

She made both of us sit on the bed in front of her, while she settled into the bean bag on the side. Taking a deep breath, she confessed, "How will it happen? I am scared just thinking about it."

"Hey Di, I'll think about it later, but first I want to know Bhaskar better," I told her. Then, turning to Divyasha, I asked, "Tell me, how and when did you find out that Bhaskar is a victim of narcissistic abuse?"

Divyasha took a deep breath and began, "Actually, I had been noticing since childhood that whatever Mummy said, Bhaskar would just bow his head and accept it without a word. Then, a few months ago, Dadi's health deteriorated significantly. Bhaskar asked Mummy for permission to go to Ajmer to take care of her. Mummy started making strange excuses, saying she couldn't stay alone at home and who would take care of them. She spoke to him very lovingly, which was unusual because she always shouted at Bhaskar. But this time, for the first time, Bhaskar mustered up the courage, packed his bags, and went to Ajmer."

She paused, her eyes reflecting the weight of her memories. "One day, Mummy called Bhaskar and said, 'You are a narcissist. Go and sleep in your mother's lap. Useless people like you should never get married. People like you are a blot on love,' and other such hurtful things. That's when I realized the extent of her control and abuse."

"Oh my god, did she really say all this?" Didi asked, her eyes wide with shock and disbelief.

"Yes, really," Divyasha confirmed, her voice steady but filled with the weight of the truth.

"Then, what happened?" Didi asked, her voice filled with concern.

Divyasha continued, "After that call, Bhaskar was devastated. He stayed in Ajmer to take care of Dadi, but he was a changed person. He became more withdrawn and quiet. It was then that I started to see the full extent of Mummy's control over him. I realized that he wasn't useless; he was just a victim of her constant manipulation and abuse And when I googled it, everything I read made me realize that Bhaskar is a victim. Mummy actually has narcissistic personality disorder," Divyasha said, her voice filled with a mix of revelation and sadness."

"Then?" I prompted, eager to hear more.

Divyasha continued, "Some signs were listed on Google, the first being an exaggerated sense of self-importance. Mummy always presented herself in an over-the-top manner. She held a good position at her job, so even if it was a small matter, she would boast about it to everyone as if the sky itself bowed down before her."

"Did she do this with everyone or was Bhaskar her only victim?" I asked, my curiosity piqued.

"She didn't spare anyone, not even me," Divyasha replied. "Sometimes I would get so worried that I felt like running away, but then I would remind myself that, despite everything, she loved me. This was why Bhaskar could never understand what was happening to him. If it had stopped there, it might not have affected Bhaskar so deeply. But along with boasting about her success, she would start demeaning Bhaskar. He would just listen silently because whenever he thought of doing something or mustered up the courage, she would say so many hurtful things that he began to see himself as the weakest of all."

"No one ever tried to explain to her that she was doing wrong?" I asked, puzzled.

Divyasha shook her head. "No, no one dared to. Mummy had such a strong personality that everyone was either too scared or too conditioned to challenge her. Even when we tried to hint at it, she would dismiss us or turn the conversation around to make it seem like we were the ones at fault. It was like walking on eggshells around her all the time."

"You never tried to explain it to her?" I asked, my voice filled with concern.

"I did try," Divyasha replied, her voice heavy with emotion. "But I was affected by her too. Sometimes, I felt like I was also a villain, just like Bhaskar. I feared that I would never be able to do anything in the future. Bhaskar never told me how he felt, but when I finally took this step, grandmother told me that before and even after marriage, Bhaskar was confident, caring, and intelligent for many years. Now, he's just a shadow of his former self, unable to muster the courage to do anything. Before the wedding, he was handsome, went to the gym every day, and was strong."

"I have seen how strong Bhaskar still is," I said confidently.

"How?" my sister asked, curiosity evident in her eyes.

"I'll tell you later," I replied, eager to hear more from Divyasha. "First, let's hear what else happened."

Then Divyasha continued, "She always used to provoke me, insisting that I dress up like her for weddings or any function. I wasn't allowed to wear clothes of my choice, and the same thing happened with Bhaskar. She always had to be on top. At first, I saw it as her way of showing love, but gradually, I started feeling suffocated. I am who I am, and I don't want to show off so much. But if someone disagreed with her, she would call them disrespectful names and make them feel so guilty that they would start doubting themselves, wondering if they were ever right. She sees herself as the center of the universe, with the rest of us as planets revolving around her. She demands devotion, respect, and unwavering attention. Anyone who doesn't comply faces her wrath, and she makes them do things they never wanted to."

Di and I exchanged glances, both of us wondering whether Bhaskar was truly human or if he was some divine incarnation. The silence was thick with our shared astonishment.

Breaking the silence, Divyasha said, "I've only told you a little bit. If I were to write a book on her character, I could fill thousands of pages with every detail."

"Let's go now, Bhaskar is also waiting, and you need to get ready for coffee this evening," Divyasha said to me as she started to leave.

After reaching the stairs, she turned back and added, "Take care of Bhaskar, Niharika. He is very scared of going into crowds now."

CHAPTER FIVE

Birthday

After Divyasha left, Di also prepared to leave the room as she had to go somewhere with Jiju. She turned to me and said, "Listen, I am leaving. You take care of yourself. Don't think too much. Sometimes God gives us something in our life that we cannot even imagine. But I promise you one thing: whatever your decision will be, Jiju and I will support you completely." She hugged me tightly, offering a comforting embrace, and then left the room.

As I lay there on the bed, my mind was a whirlwind of thoughts, questioning whether what I was doing was right or wrong. The saying "a blind man sees everything green during the monsoon season" perfectly described my state of mind. All I could see was my love for Bhaskar, but the future felt uncertain and shrouded in mystery.

Feeling worried, I turned to God and prayed, "Oh my Shivji, please show me a way. I know you will not let me do anything wrong." With full faith in my heart, I remembered my Shivji and lay down on the bed, hoping for guidance and clarity.

When I couldn't sleep despite tossing and turning for what felt like hours, I got up and went to the balcony, settling into a chair. I felt like listening to songs, but as a psychology student, I knew that in my current emotional state, I would gravitate towards romantic love songs, which would only heighten my excitement. So, I decided against it. Bhaskar and I were supposed to meet at 4 PM, and there were still 2 hours left.

So much was going on in my mind that I thought I should smoke a cigarette. I went down to the panwadi in front of the colony, bought a cigarette, and started smoking.

Then, an old man approached me. He looked like a gentleman and was quite handsome too. He sat next to me and asked, "Can you give me your cigarette? I want to light mine."

I said, "Grandpa, should I go and get a lighter for you?"

He smiled warmly, his eyes twinkling with a hint of mischief. "No, I could have done that myself, but I had a purpose in asking you."

Curiosity and confusion swirled within me. "What is that?" I asked, my brow furrowing deeply. For a fleeting moment, a shadow of doubt crossed my mind, making me wonder if the old man had some hidden, unsavory motive. But what he said next would forever change my perspective on life.

"Sometimes ask Bhaskar when his birthday is," he said, his voice gentle yet filled with an enigmatic weight.

His words struck me like a bolt of lightning. I felt a jolt of realization and awe. I stood up abruptly, my heart pounding in my chest. How did he know Bhaskar? The environment seemed to blur around me as the significance of his message began to sink in. Until that moment, I had believed in the existence of God, but I had never imagined that divine guidance could come in such an unexpected form.

"Don't worry, I have to tell you a lot now," he said, his voice steady and reassuring as he held my hand and gently guided me back to my seat.

I was at a loss for words, so I decided to listen quietly, my mind racing with questions.

"When I came here in this suit and boots, nothing happened to you," he began, his eyes searching mine for understanding. "And even after seeing Bhaskar in such a bad state, you could not control yourself. Have you ever thought why?" he asked, his tone both probing and compassionate.

His question hung in the air, heavy with meaning. I felt a mix of confusion and anticipation, my heart pounding as I waited for him to reveal the deeper truth behind his words.

There was something different about him, as if his eyes had hypnotized me. Everything around me seemed to blur. I said, "I don't know, Dada, but I was getting drawn towards him, maybe because he is handsome and I am young."

He chuckled softly, a knowing smile playing on his lips. "I am also handsome and I look even better than him, but nothing happened to you on seeing me, why?" he asked, his gaze piercing yet gentle.

I had no answer to this question, so I kept quiet and just shrugged my shoulders, feeling a mix of embarrassment and confusion.

"Whatever Bhaskar suffered in his life was his karma, and he had to end it. That's why he met Ayesha and all that happened," he explained, his voice filled with a profound sense of understanding and compassion. "But now the time has come to end the sorrow from his life, and you are the charioteer of Bhaskar's life."

His words resonated deeply within me, filling me with a sense of purpose and responsibility. The weight of his message settled on my shoulders, and I realized that my role in Bhaskar's life was far more significant than I had ever imagined.

"Why, how, when, where—Bhole Baba himself will give you answers to all these questions when the time comes. Troubles will come, but you should not be disappointed because this meeting has been decided by destiny itself." As he was telling me all this, a ball suddenly came and hit my hand.

I turned, ready to scold the child who had thrown it, but to my astonishment, the grandfather had vanished. The child approached, picked up his ball, and with a mischievous smile, said, "Keep in mind what I have said." Then he ran off, leaving me in a state of bewilderment.

I turned back to the paan vendor and asked, "Where did the uncle who was sitting with me go?"

He looked at me, puzzled. "I don't know, Didi. You have been sitting alone for so long, and I haven't seen anyone else."

A chill ran down my spine as I realized the gravity of what had just happened. Had I imagined it all? Or had I just experienced something truly extraordinary? The words of the grandfather echoed in my mind, filling me with a sense of destiny and purpose that I couldn't quite comprehend yet.

It felt like the ground slipped from under my feet and the sky had fallen on my head. I ran back home, my mind racing with the words that uncle had said to me. Strangely, ever since I returned, all my fear and anxiety had vanished, replaced by a calm determination.

As the time to meet Bhaskar approached, I quickly got ready, donning the suit my sister had given me. I headed straight to Bhaskar's house, arriving with 12 minutes to spare before 4 o'clock. Bhaskar was already prepared, thanks to Divyasha, who had picked out some nice clothes for him. In black jeans and a loose-fit t-shirt, he looked no older than 38.

As he went inside to put on his shoes, I seized the moment and asked Divyasha, "When is Bhaskar's birthday?"

"23 Feb 1971 ," Divyasha told me before heading inside.

Curious, I quickly googled the significance of this date and was stunned to discover that it was Maha Shivratri. Since childhood, I have had unshakable faith in Lord Shiva and worship Him with all my heart every day. The amazing thing was that I was also born on Maha Shivratri in 2001.

As I connected the dots, the words of that Baba began to make sense. It felt as if a divine plan was unfolding before me. Bhaskar and I were destined to be together, our relationship ordained in heaven. This love, I realized, could never be wrong.

We both arrived at a charming café that Sarika Di had recommended. The ambiance was perfect—quiet and serene, just the way Bhaskar liked it. I found the most secluded corner and sat there with Bhaskar, the seating arranged so we could sit face to face.

Sensing his discomfort, I gently placed my hand on his and said, "Don't worry, I am with you."

He kept his head bowed, his voice soft and hesitant. "Ask me whatever else you want to ask," he said, still not meeting my eyes.

I could feel the weight of his emotions, and I knew this moment was crucial for both of us. Taking a deep breath, I prepared to ask the questions that had been on my mind, hoping to bring us closer and understand the depths of his heart.

"Nothing, I don't want to know anything more now, I just want to tell you," I said, just as a waiter approached.

He placed the menu card in front of Bhaskar and greeted us. I greeted him back, but Bhaskar remained silent. The waiter left the menu card and walked away.

Noticing that Bhaskar wasn't touching the menu card, I picked it up and asked, "What would you like to eat?"

"I don't want to eat anything, but I am very thirsty. Can you get me water?" Bhaskar replied, his voice soft and distant.

I nodded and called the waiter over, asking him to bring water. I also ordered white sauce pasta and two fresh lime sodas, hoping the refreshing drinks would help ease Bhaskar's discomfort. As we waited, I could feel the tension slowly dissipating, replaced by a sense of calm and understanding between us.

"Now tell me what you were saying," I prompted Bhaskar.

"I was not saying anything, you were going to say something," he replied, his voice tinged with confusion.

I hesitated for a moment before speaking, "Bhaskar, did you ever think that you would love someone else or leave that woman and become someone else's?"

He looked down, his hands trembling slightly. "No, because by the time I understood why this was happening, I was completely shattered. The truth is, I have lost all faith in love," Bhaskar said nervously.

His words hung heavy in the air, and I could feel the depth of his pain. I wanted to reach out and reassure him, to let him know that love could still be a source of healing and hope.

"And now, now that you are free, you can think of loving a girl?" I asked him with great hope.

"Now who will love me? I am an old man and I no longer have that charm which girls used to love at one time," Bhaskar replied, his voice tinged with sadness.

I blushed slightly and said, "Why, you still have that charm that any girl would be ready to die for you."

A slight smile appeared on Bhaskar's face, but it quickly faded. He started sobbing, tears streaming down his cheeks.

"What happened, Bhaskar?" I asked, my heart aching for him.

He struggled to speak through his tears. "It's just... I never thought I could feel this way again. The pain, the betrayal... it all feels so fresh. But your words, they give me hope, and that scares me."

I squeezed his hand gently, trying to offer comfort. "It's okay to feel scared, Bhaskar. But you deserve happiness and love. You deserve to heal."

He looked up at me, his eyes filled with a mix of vulnerability and gratitude. "Thank you," he whispered. "Thank you for believing in me."

He was getting nervous and couldn't say anything. At first, I thought I had made a mistake by bringing him here, but then an aunty sitting nearby noticed his tears. She got up and approached us, her presence warm and comforting.

"Every life has two aspects, one is good and the other is bad. Time does not remain the same in anyone's life. I have gone through a bad phase, but today I have forgotten that old life and have started a new one. I am the owner of this cafe, and not only food but stories are also made here," she said with a gentle smile.

"Stories, you mean?" I asked, intrigued by her words.

She nodded, her eyes sparkling with wisdom. "Yes, stories of hope, resilience, and new beginnings. Everyone who comes here brings a piece of their life, and sometimes, sharing those stories helps heal old wounds and create new paths."

Bhaskar looked up, his tears slowly subsiding. The aunty's words seemed to resonate with him, offering a glimmer of hope. I squeezed his hand gently, feeling a renewed sense of optimism for both of us.

"Yes, look at the stories," she said, pointing towards a wall adorned with pictures of couples. "They all came here with problems in their lives. Just like he is crying, I have seen many lovers crying here."

Bhaskar, still emotional, quickly interjected, "We don't love each other, ma'am. You have misunderstood. She is my doctor and is treating my madness." His voice trailed off as he became silent again.

The aunty smiled kindly, undeterred by his words. "Sometimes, healing comes in unexpected forms. Whether it's love or care, what matters is the connection and the support we give each other."

I squeezed Bhaskar's hand gently, hoping to convey that I was there for him, no matter what. The aunty's words lingered in the air, offering a sense of comfort and understanding. It felt like a tsunami had crashed into my awakening hopes with Bhaskar's words. Desperately, I looked at the aunty, hoping she would say something to save the sinking boat of my love.

"Oh, I am sorry I disturbed you," she said, starting to leave. But before she walked away, she stopped and placed a comforting hand on my shoulder. "I am never wrong. There is something between you two that is different and much more than just a doctor-patient relationship," she said with a knowing smile, then returned to her chair.

Her words lingered in the air, offering a glimmer of hope. I looked at Bhaskar, who seemed lost in thought, and felt a renewed sense of determination. Maybe, just maybe, there was a chance for us after all.

I wish Bhaskar would understand this soon, but looking at him, it doesn't seem like he is going to realize it on his own. I knew I would have to do something special to make him see that I love him, but first, I needed to help him move past the memories of that woman.

For now, I decided to focus on Bhaskar and asked, "Tell me something about yourself and your life before marriage. You are so handsome now, you must have created a stir earlier. Did you never have a girlfriend?"

Bhaskar looked up, a faint smile playing on his lips as he reminisced. "Well, before marriage, life was quite different. I was always busy with work and studies, but yes, there were a few girls who caught my eye. However, I never had a serious girlfriend. I guess I was too focused on my career and responsibilities."

His eyes softened as he spoke, and I could see a glimpse of the man he used to be, full of dreams and ambitions. It was a small step, but it felt like we were beginning to bridge the gap between his past and the possibility of a new future.

"I was in school when I understood the meaning of love for the first time. She was my neighbor and we both grew up playing together since childhood. She used to call my mother bua (aunt), so we both had never seen each other in this way. And one day I saw her friend at a wedding. She was cute. So I asked Devika to give me her number. It was the first time we had talked about something like this. Otherwise, we mostly used to talk about studies or sports and sometimes household matters. I still remember when I asked her for a number. She told me that she thought I was very simple. So I said, I am simple, are you going to give me her number or not? She said, okay, I will ask her and then the next day, her friend started talking to me from her phone saying that I don't have a phone." And saying this, Bhaskar started laughing. He had forgotten his fear while telling his first love story.

"What happened next?" I asked

"Then slowly I started talking to Devika more and forgot about her friend," he said

"Then why didn't you marry your Devika?" I asked

"At that time I was also a child and neither of us could understand properly whether it was love or just attraction," he said and started smiling.

Seeing his laughter, I felt that if Devika had to be brought back to make him laugh, then I would stand by the side and keep watching Devika and Bhaskar laughing and laughing all my life.

"Still something must have happened that you two got separated," I asked

"Yes, when her father found out, he snatched her phone and sent her to her aunt's place for studies. The same thing happened to me; my phone was taken away, and I was told to focus on my studies. We couldn't talk to each other anymore. During that time, I met Ayesha, and you already know what happened next." He fell silent after saying this and then asked, "Do you mind if I smoke a cigarette? If you want to join me, that would be even better."

"No, I've had enough for today. You go ahead and smoke, I'll wait here," I replied. Bhaskar got up and headed to the smoking zone.

I got up and walked over to sit beside that aunty. When she asked me what was wrong, I poured out the entire story to her. In short, her words deeply reinforced my belief.

"Have you ever wondered what emotions a priest experiences when he performs a puja?" she asked. "Can we feel the same way about another human being? Most would say no, but I believe otherwise. When a priest surrenders himself with pure love before the idol of God, he doesn't think about anyone else. He doesn't worry about what the world will say or how insignificant he might seem in front of the divine. He doesn't question whether his love will be reciprocated. In that moment, he forgets everything and simply loves his God with all his heart."

"Is love worship, aunty?" I asked, my voice tinged with curiosity and a hint of confusion.

"This is how love is, Niharika. If you feel this way for Bhaskar, then you are on the right path. Don't let society, or your thoughts influenced by society, or any other emotion come between your love and Bhaskar. Love is the purest feeling that connects one soul to another. There is no place for lies in love. As long as truth is alive, love is alive. The day truth is murdered, understand that love will also end that day," she said, her voice filled with wisdom and warmth.

"Does a person who truly loves never lie?" I asked, my voice trembling with uncertainty.

"A man tells a hundred lies every day, sometimes to hide his failures, sometimes to find peace amidst the chaos of life. But there is always one person in front of whom he is completely truthful—the person connected to his soul, the one he loves. Lies have a short lifespan; they fade away quickly. On the other hand, truth is eternal, living on for centuries. If you feel such truth for Bhaskar, and if Bhaskar holds that same truth in his heart for you, then nothing can stop your union. One day, you will see that even God will come to unite you with your truth," she replied, her words resonating with profound wisdom and hope.

Bhaskar was about to return. The smoking zone was made of glass, so he could see us, and we could see him. As soon as I saw him approaching, I quickly said goodbye to Aunty and returned to my seat. Bhaskar also came back and settled into his place.

"What was that aunty saying to you?" Bhaskar asked, curiosity evident in his eyes as he sat down.

"She was just talking about me, nothing important. Let's leave that aside and talk about you. So far, I've only heard good things about you, but now I want to know the real you—the truths we usually keep hidden. There must be some flaws, some bad things too. I want to know about them," I said, gently holding his hand.

"Yes, like every human being, I have my share of flaws. I used to get very angry—not every day, but when I did, I wouldn't care about anything. I would be ready to lash out, almost as if I was ready to kill. My biggest shortcoming, which I've never told anyone until now, was my intense jealousy. There was a time when I had big dreams and ambitions, and that jealousy consumed me. But with the blessings of my Lord Shiva, I managed to overcome it," Bhaskar confessed, his voice tinged with a mix of vulnerability and relief.

"And, is there anything else?" I asked, looking deeply into his eyes. I could sense there was more he wanted to share, something weighing on his heart.

Bhaskar hesitated before continuing, "Another major shortcoming was my obsession with sex. I used to think too much about passionate lovemaking with the one I loved. Maybe God has punished me for that. I could never control the intense desire, and that desperation consumed my mind," he confessed openly, his voice filled with a mix of guilt and vulnerability.

Then he said, "I'm truly sorry, Niharika. I might have spoken too much. My intention was never to make you uncomfortable. It just came out in the flow, and I ended up saying more than I should have. I don't know why, but I feel this overwhelming need to be honest with you, to share everything—whether it's clean or messy. I just want to unburden myself of all the thoughts I've kept bottled up until now."

Bhaskar shared everything about himself with me, without a hint of hesitation or concealment. This honesty drew me closer to him. Everyone has flaws, but a person who acknowledges them can never deceive anyone. The waiter arrived with pasta and fresh lime soda, along with a note that read, "Zindagi na milegi dobara." When I glanced back, the aunty winked at me and gave me a thumbs-up, wishing me all the best. She then settled into the same seat and began reading her book, the cover of which bore the title "Maha Shivratri."

As I served pasta onto Bhaskar's plate, I casually asked, "When is your birthday?"

"February 23rd, 1971," he replied.

"Was there anything special about that day?" I inquired, hoping to keep the conversation flowing, even though Divyasha had already filled me in.

"Yes, it was Maha Shivratri," he said with a smile. "And the funny thing is, everyone used to call me Bhola when I was a kid."

"Can I share something interesting with you?" I asked Bhaskar, feeling a mix of excitement and shyness.

"Yes, please do," he encouraged me.

"I was also born on Maha Shivaratri, on February 21st, 2001," I revealed with a smile, feeling a bit bashful.

"Oh, really? Wow, that's amazing! No wonder I feel such a strong connection with you," he responded warmly.

He was quietly eating pasta, looking as innocent as a child, and I couldn't help but watch him. I felt an overwhelming urge to share what was in my heart, but I couldn't summon the courage. It wasn't the fear of what the world might think of me or that Bhaskar might misunderstand me; rather, I was terrified that revealing my feelings might push him away. I feared he might retreat back into the darkness from which I had gently guided him out, holding his hand.

It was getting late, and we needed to head home, so we left the café and started waiting for a cab. However, due to the rain, no cabs were available.

"Let's go for a walk, shall we?" Bhaskar suggested.

"In the rain?" I asked, a bit surprised.

"Yes, don't you like getting wet in the rain?" he asked with a playful smile.

"It's not a bad idea anyway," I said, deciding to go along with it. We had barely taken two steps, already getting drenched in the rain, when my phone rang.

When I answered the phone, a man's voice on the other end asked, "Where do you want to go, Madam?"

"I don't know where I want to go now, but I feel my destination is close by. Wrong number." With that, I hung up the phone and continued walking with Bhaskar.

"What do you hate the most?" I asked, hoping to keep the conversation flowing.

"I cannot tolerate lies," he replied. "It's not that I've never lied in my life, but there's a limit. When a lie causes harm to someone, it inflicts wounds so deep that no medicine can heal them."

"Like your relationship with Ayesha," I blurted out. I hadn't really thought it through, but now I felt that I had the right to say anything to Bhaskar. I knew he wouldn't mind.

"I will serve your parents all my life, I will build your house, and I don't know what kind of dangerous lies she used to tell. When I think about it today, I get so angry at myself," Bhaskar said, his voice tinged with frustration. He pulled out a cigarette from his pocket and lit it, the glow of the flame briefly illuminating his face.

"What is your fault in this? Stop blaming yourself," I said, extending my hand towards him and asking for a cigarette. He started to hand me a new one from his pocket, but I stopped him. "No, we will share," I insisted. He took a long drag, then handed me the cigarette, the smoke curling between us like a silent promise.

While sharing those cigarettes, we finally reached home. A thought crossed my mind: I wished that, just as we shared this cigarette, we could share everything in life. With this thought lingering, I said, "We've reached home, and it's time to go. I wish this moment could last forever, and we could keep sharing every thought and every emotion like this."

"I don't feel like going either, but I have to," Bhaskar said, taking the last drag of his cigarette before crushing the bud under his foot. "Thank you. Once again, because of you, I understand my responsibilities. I promise I will give Divyasha the good life she deserves, the one she lost because of me. Now, you should go too; everyone will be waiting for you at home. Bye."

"Don't say bye, say we will meet again. It gives hope to the person leaving, a promise that they'll reunite with the one they love and cherish," I said.

"Ok, we will meet again," Bhaskar said with a warm smile. He then opened the door to his house and stepped inside.

As I came home, my thoughts were consumed by the complexities of love. Sometimes it brings pain, other times it brings peace. My days are filled with thoughts of him, and my nights are spent in his memory. Today, I want to confess: I want to stay, to reside in your heart. My days are restless, my nights are thirsty. I don't want to feel this restlessness for even a moment longer. Let there be one heart, one life, one destination. Let us become each other's companions. Understand the state of my heart, my love. I won't say it out loud; I have my limits. He doesn't know the turmoil within me. Oh Bhaskar, you are so simple. There's a fragrance of loyalty in your innocence. Why shouldn't I sacrifice everything for it? My desperate heart tells me to embrace your shadow. This meeting of ours feels like a divine plan.

CHAPTER SIX

Encounter

With the memories of these moments spent with Bhaskar, one thought kept echoing in my mind: as long as Ayesha remained a part of Bhaskar's life, I could never truly be in it. That night, before drifting off to sleep, I made a firm decision. Ayesha would have to be removed from Bhaskar's life, because even today, she was still his wife.

The next morning, I began my search for a divorce lawyer, but so far, I hadn't found the right person to help me. Feeling disappointed, I stood on the balcony, thinking of Bhole Baba. Just then, I saw Anand Jiju approaching. Sarika Di was still asleep, so I went to open the gate and informed him that Di was still sleeping. During our conversation, he noticed my worried expression and asked, "What happened? You seem a bit troubled."

With slight hesitation, I confided, "Jiju, I have a friend whose wife is causing him a lot of trouble. I've been looking for a divorce lawyer, but I haven't found anyone who can handle this case."

"Your friend's name is Bhaskar, right?" he asked, and my face turned pale. Noticing my reaction, Jiju quickly reassured me, "Don't worry, your sister has told me everything. I will do something." With that, he took out his phone and walked towards the gate, already deep in conversation.

After talking on the phone for a while, he came back and sat on the sofa. "Your work will be done," he assured me. "I'll give you a number. Talk to him and explain all your problems. He will surely help you." He then forwarded the number to me.

Without wasting any time, I called the number and, sitting there in front of Jiju, I explained everything. After listening to my story, the person on the other end promised to help and said he would call back in half an hour before disconnecting.

Jiju looked at me seriously and said, "If you want to help Bhaskar, the first step is to contact that woman. What's her name?"

"Ayesha," I replied.

"We should call Ayesha or meet her in person to find out more about her," Jiju suggested.

"But why would she agree to meet me or reveal the truth?" I asked, feeling uncertain.

"In my opinion, the best approach is to record a call with Bhaskar and have him provoke her. But do you think Bhaskar would be willing to do this?" Jiju asked, his concern evident.

"No, he's not in a condition to cleverly flirt with her and provoke her. We'll have to think of something else," I told Jiju.

We were both deep in thought when we heard Didi's voice. We went upstairs to her room.

"You're here?" Didi said to Jiju.

"I came much earlier, but you were asleep. So, we sat down and started talking," Jiju replied, hugging Sarika Di before sitting beside her.

"Okay, I am leaving," I said, starting to head back downstairs.

"Hey, I want to talk to you. Come and sit," Jiju called out.

"I had called him to clear your confusion. Sit and gain some knowledge," Didi added.

"Now tell me, did the conversation progress any further yesterday?" Didi asked, since by the time she came home, I had already fallen asleep.

"It did, but from my side, the score is still zero," I admitted.

Before I could say anything more, my phone rang. It was the lawyer whose number Jiju had given me.

"Jiju, the call has come," I informed him and got up to take the call. While I was on the phone, Jiju filled Didi in on everything.

After the call, I returned with a smile and excitedly told my brother-in-law and sister, "Mahesh Sir will help us with the divorce." Didi and Jiju were thrilled to hear this. Didi hugged me tightly and said, "I am proud of you."

"What did Mahesh Sir say?" Jiju asked, curious about the details.

"They said we can free the victim on medical grounds, but we need someone's testimony," I explained to Jiju. I then invited Divyasha to Sarika Di's house, as we needed both her consent and testimony to help Bhaskar.

As soon as Divyasha arrived, I told her everything. She started dancing with joy.

"Can this really happen, Niharika?" she asked, her eyes filled with hope.

"Yes, just get ready and, if possible, prepare Bhaskar well for this case," I advised her.

"Leave that to me. I will make Bhaskar understand," Divyasha assured me confidently.

From that moment onwards, we provided all the details of the case, and whatever Mahesh Sir asked for, we promptly delivered. After a discussion with Mahesh Sir, Divyasha held my hand as we walked towards the door. Just before heading to her house, she asked, "Can I call you mom now?"

"You are absolutely crazy, go away," I replied with a smile. After closing the gate, I couldn't help but laugh to myself. Her words made me feel as if a sitar had started playing in my mind, and I just wanted to dance to that tune. But then I remembered that there were still many challenges ahead, and I shouldn't be too happy just yet.

Jiju, Sarika Di, and I spent the entire day at Mahesh Sir's house, running around to get everything in order. Finally, the papers were ready. We sent a copy to Ayesha, and since the case was to be heard in the Ajmer court, a summons was also sent to her. In the evening, I went to Bhaskar's house to deliver the papers. After explaining everything to Divyasha, I left without meeting Bhaskar. I really wanted to see him, but I feared he might be upset by all this. I couldn't bear to see him sad, not even for a moment.

Divyasha had emotionally prepared Bhaskar for the case, and Ayesha had also arrived in Ajmer. Finally, the hearing began. On one side, Ayesha stood armed with all her defenses, while on the other, we were focused solely on how to save Bhaskar. But hats off to Mahesh Sir's skills. After thoroughly studying narcissistic behavior, he crafted such an intricate trap that Ayesha found herself hopelessly ensnared.

Judge: We will now hear the testimony from Bhaskar's advocate. Please proceed.

Mahesh Sir: Thank you, Your Honor. Ayesha has always been very controlling and cunning. She often twists the truth to suit her story.

Ayesha: (interrupting, with a sharp tone) That's not true! I always have to clean up his mess. He's just trying to make me look bad.

Judge: (firmly) Ayesha, please let him finish.

Mahesh Sir: (resuming with a calm but firm voice) As I was saying, she would often put down Bhaskar in front of his friends and family, which over time made Bhaskar feel worthless. Ayesha always needed to be the center of attention.

Ayesha: (smirking, her eyes glinting with a mix of defiance and amusement) Maybe if you were more competent, I wouldn't have to step in all the time.

Judge: (sternly, with a hint of impatience) Ayesha, please refrain from making such comments.

Mahesh Sir: (taking a deep breath, his voice steady but laced with frustration) Ayesha also has a habit of exaggerating her achievements and downplaying those of others. For example, once she took credit for a project at work on which Bhaskar had done most of the work.

Ayesha: (defensively, her tone rising as she leans forward, eyes blazing) I was the one who led the team! Without my leadership, nothing would have been accomplished.

The tension in the courtroom is palpable, each word exchanged like a spark in a tinderbox, threatening to ignite the simmering emotions of everyone present. The judge's gavel, a symbol of order, seems almost powerless against the raw human drama unfolding before it. Spectators hold their breath, caught in the gripping narrative of accusation and defense, each side presenting their truth with unwavering conviction.

Judge: (with a firm, authoritative tone) Ayesha, this is Bhaskar's testimony. You will have your turn to speak.

Mahesh Sir: (his voice steady, but with a hint of sadness) She never shows any sympathy. When Bhaskar's father was ill, instead of showing any concern for Bhaskar or Bhaskar's father, she would complain about how inconvenient it was causing her.

Ayesha: (rolling her eyes dramatically, her voice dripping with sarcasm) Oh please, I had my own problems to deal with. I can't be expected to handle everyone else's issues too.

Judge: (leaning forward, eyes narrowing) Ayesha, your lack of empathy and constant need to assert dominance are concerning. Mahesh, do you have any more examples?

The courtroom is thick with tension, every word exchanged adding to the charged atmosphere. The judge's voice cuts through the air like a knife, attempting to maintain order amidst the emotional storm. Mahesh Sir's calm demeanor contrasts sharply with Ayesha's defensive and dismissive attitude, painting a vivid picture of the strained dynamics at play. Spectators watch with bated breath, the drama unfolding before them more gripping than any fiction.

Mahesh Sir: (nodding solemnly, his voice steady and clear) Yes, Honorable. She often misleads Bhaskar, making him question his reality. She would deny everything she said or did, even when my client Bhaskar had proof.

Ayesha: (laughing dismissively, her eyes sparkling with a mix of amusement and disdain) He is just too sensitive. He always blows things out of proportion.

The courtroom falls silent, the weight of Ayesha's words hanging in the air. Her laughter, cold and unfeeling, echoes through the room, a stark contrast to the gravity of the accusations. The judge's gaze sharpens, reflecting a growing concern over Ayesha's apparent lack of empathy.

Judge: (leaning forward, his voice firm and unyielding) Ayesha, your lack of empathy and constant need to assert dominance are concerning. Mahesh, do you have any more examples?

Mahesh Sir: (taking a deep breath, his expression resolute) Yes, Honorable. She often misleads Bhaskar, making him question his reality. She would deny everything she said or did, even when my client Bhaskar had proof.

Ayesha: (laughing again, her tone dripping with condescension) He is just too sensitive. He always blows things out of proportion.

The tension in the room is palpable, each word exchanged like a spark in a tinderbox, threatening to ignite the simmering emotions of everyone present. The judge's gavel, a symbol of order, seems almost powerless against the raw human drama unfolding before it. Spectators hold their breath, caught in the gripping narrative of accusation and defense, each side presenting their truth with unwavering conviction.

Judge: (turning to Ayesha's defense lawyer) You may now question Bhaskar.

A hush falls over the courtroom as Ayesha's defense lawyer rises, the anticipation thick in the air. The uncertainty of what will happen next grips everyone, a collective tension that binds the room in a moment of shared anxiety.

The resolute support of me and Divyasha was a beacon of comfort for Bhaskar during the grueling process of his divorce. Ayesha's devious strategies grew increasingly frantic, but Bhaskar's determination remained unshaken. He realized that his happiness and well-being were pursuits worth fighting for, and with each passing day, he felt more empowered to reclaim his life.

With my youthful joy and sincere love, I became a ray of hope for Bhaskar. I provided him with the security and affection he had long yearned for, standing by his side through court appearances and periods of emotional turmoil. My presence was a constant reminder that he was not alone in this battle.

Divyasha, with her unwavering support, played a crucial role in reminding her father of his worth and the brighter days that lay ahead. Her gentle reassurances and steadfast belief in his strength helped Bhaskar see the light at the end of the tunnel. Together, we formed a shield of love and support around him, making him feel capable of overcoming any obstacle.

As the days turned into weeks, Bhaskar's confidence grew. He began to see a future where he was free from

Ayesha's manipulative grasp, a future where he could find peace and happiness. Our collective support was the foundation upon which he rebuilt his life, one step at a time.

Defense Lawyer: (standing tall, with a piercing gaze) Thank you, Your Honor. Bhaskar, I have a few questions for you. You mentioned that Ayesha humiliated you in front of friends and family. Can you give any specific examples?

Bhaskar took a deep breath, his eyes momentarily flickering with uncertainty. But then, he glanced at Divyasha, her eyes filled with unwavering support, and at me, my expression radiating hope and encouragement. In that moment, he felt a surge of courage.

Bhaskar: (his voice steadying as he spoke) Yes, there were many instances. One time, during a family gathering, Ayesha openly mocked my career choices, calling me a failure in front of everyone. She laughed at my efforts and made me feel insignificant.

The courtroom was silent, every eye fixed on Bhaskar as he continued, his voice growing stronger with each word. He was no longer just recounting his past; he was reclaiming his dignity.

Bhaskar: (with a newfound resolve) Another time, at a friend's wedding, she belittled me in front of our friends, saying I was incapable of making any decisions on my own. It was humiliating and deeply hurtful.

As Bhaskar spoke, he kept his gaze on Divyasha and me, drawing strength from our presence. The fear that had once gripped him was now replaced by a fierce determination. He knew that after today, there would be no one standing between him and the life he deserved.

The defense lawyer, sensing the shift in Bhaskar's demeanor, paused for a moment, taken aback by the intensity of his testimony. The judge watched intently, recognizing the significance of this moment for Bhaskar.

Bhaskar: (his voice trembling slightly as he recalls the painful memories) Yes, once it happened at a family function too. Ayesha called me unfit in front of everyone because I had forgotten to bring a utensil. It may seem small to say or hear, but for a husband to hear disrespectful words from his wife in front of everyone, it shakes the soul. And this didn't happen just once, but repeatedly, every day, over every little matter.

Bhaskar paused, his eyes reflecting the deep hurt he had endured. The courtroom was silent, the weight of his words hanging heavily in the air.

Bhaskar: (continuing, his voice growing stronger with each word) I started forgetting that I am a human being. I started forgetting that I was ever respected. When I confronted Ayesha, she told me that no one ever respected me. She gave me many examples of things I had forgotten, and hearing all those things that had hurt me, I started breaking down.

The raw emotion in Bhaskar's voice was palpable, each word a testament to the pain he had endured. He glanced at Divyasha and me, drawing strength from our unwavering support. The fear that had once gripped him was now replaced by a fierce determination to reclaim his dignity.

The defense lawyer, sensing the gravity of Bhaskar's testimony, paused, allowing the weight of his words to settle over the courtroom. The judge watched intently, recognizing the significance of this moment for Bhaskar.

Defense Lawyer: (leaning forward, his voice calm but probing) And how did you respond to that?

Bhaskar: (his voice tinged with embarrassment) I was embarrassed and tried to explain that I had been busy with work, but she wouldn't listen.

Defense Lawyer: (raising an eyebrow) So, you admit that you forgot something important. Isn't it possible that Ayesha was simply frustrated and expressed it poorly?

Bhaskar: (shaking his head, his voice firm) It wasn't just frustration. It was a pattern of behavior.

Defense Lawyer: (nodding slightly) You also mentioned that Ayesha took credit for a project at work. Did you ever discuss this with her or your superiors?

Bhaskar: (sighing, his frustration evident) I tried to, but she always managed to twist the situation to her advantage.

Defense Lawyer: (with a hint of skepticism) Isn't it true that in a team setting, leadership often involves taking credit for the team's success?

Bhaskar: (nodding reluctantly) Yes, but she didn't acknowledge my contributions at all.

Defense Lawyer: (changing tactics) Regarding your father's illness, you said Ayesha complained about the inconvenience. Did she ever help in any way during that time?

Bhaskar: (hesitating, then speaking softly) She did some things, but it was minimal and always with complaints.

Defense Lawyer: (pressing on) So, she did help, despite her complaints. Isn't it possible that she was under stress as well?

Bhaskar: (shrugging, his voice weary) Maybe, but it didn't feel like she cared.

Defense Lawyer: (leaning in, his voice low and intense) Finally, you mentioned gaslighting. Can you provide a specific example where Ayesha denied something she said or did?

Bhaskar: (his voice steady, but filled with pain) There was a time she promised to attend an important event with me but later denied ever making that promise.

Defense Lawyer: (with a slight smirk) Could it be that she genuinely forgot or had a different recollection of the conversation?

Bhaskar: (shaking his head firmly) It happened too often to be just forgetfulness.

Defense Lawyer: (straightening up, his tone final) Thank you, Bhaskar. No further questions, Your Honor.

The courtroom was silent, the tension thick in the air. Bhaskar's testimony had laid bare the emotional turmoil he had endured, and the defense lawyer's probing questions had only served to highlight the depth of his pain. As Bhaskar looked at Divyasha and me, he felt a surge of hope. Today, he had spoken his truth, and with our support, he knew he could face whatever came next.

Ayesha often leans back in her chair with her arms crossed, which indicates she is defensive. She often answers questions in a sharp voice, trying to deflect blame and justify her actions. Ayesha shows clear signs of irritation, rolling her eyes, sighing loudly, and tapping her fingers impatiently. She seems frustrated by the questioning and the need to defend herself. Despite her irritation, Ayesha maintains a confident posture.

She sits upright and makes direct eye contact with Mahesh Sir, to establish control of the situation. Ayesha often dismisses Mahesh Sir's claims with a grin or laughter, which shows that she does not take his allegations seriously. She often teases Mahesh Sir, trying to downplay the seriousness of his work. When Ayesha is confronted with specific evidence or pointed questions, she gives vague or evasive answers.

She tries to divert the focus from herself to Bhaskar or other external factors. Ayesha tries to manipulate the story by distorting the facts and presenting herself as the victim. She uses persuasive language to sway the judge and jury to her side.

The court case was difficult, with many moments of uncertainty and annoyance. But Bhaskar's resolve remained unwavering. He understood that the only way he could fully live again was to release himself from Ayesha's grip. Bhaskar's fortitude was put to the test in the courtroom, but with my support and Divyasha's, he met each obstacle head-on.

Overall, Ayesha's behavior during the cross-examination reflected her narcissistic traits – defensiveness, irritability, confidence, dismissiveness, evasiveness, patience, and manipulation.

Eventually, the day arrived when Bhaskar won the case in front of the court. A wave of liberty overcame him when the divorce was granted. After Ayesha's manipulations were undone, Bhaskar had a renewed feeling of independence. Now he could see himself freed from the chains of the past in the future. Also, the court ruled that keeping the case in mind, Bhaskar will get a job in the government sector based on his profile, and whatever money he will have to spend to come out of this trauma will be borne by the government. The court asked Ayesha to pay a fine of Rs 10 lakh to Bhaskar for mental torture and appointed a government psychologist where she could go for her treatment and receive therapy.

Now that the court case was over, Bhaskar and I started a new adventure together. Based on a foundation of love, respect, and understanding, our partnership flourished. We enjoyed each other's company, supported one other's aspirations, and treasured the small moments.

Witnessing her father prosper brought satisfaction to Divyasha as well. The three of us developed a closer relationship that resulted in a loving, caring family dynamic. Bhaskar's path served as a monument to the strength of love and the ability to resist coercion and exploitation.

The courtroom drama had finally come to an end, but the emotional turmoil within me was far from over. Bhaskar, now free from Ayesha's manipulative grasp, still remained unaware of the depth of my feelings for him. As I stood there, the weight of unspoken words pressed heavily on my heart.

Tomorrow was Sarika Di's engagement function, a joyous occasion that would bring my family together in Ajmer. My parents were arriving, and amidst the celebrations, I found myself lost in a whirlwind of emotions. The thought of confessing my love to Bhaskar filled me with both hope and fear.

I had been his steadfast support through the darkest times, but now, as the dust settled, I wondered if I would ever find the courage to reveal my true feelings. The uncertainty of what lay ahead gnawed at me. Would Bhaskar see me as more than just a friend? Could our bond transform into something deeper?

As I pondered these questions, I realized that tomorrow might be the perfect opportunity to open my heart. Surrounded by loved ones and the warmth of family, perhaps I could find the strength to tell Bhaskar how much he meant to me. The journey had been long and arduous, but maybe, just maybe, it was leading us to a new beginning.

The sun was setting, casting a warm, golden hue over the city as Bhaskar and I walked back to the same cozy café where we had shared so many conversations. The familiar aroma of freshly brewed coffee greeted us as we stepped inside, and we chose a quiet corner by the window, away from the bustling crowd.

"Now you are not feeling scared, right Bhaskar?" I asked, my voice gentle but filled with concern.

Bhaskar looked at me, his eyes reflecting a mix of relief and gratitude. "As long as you and Divyasha stand with me, I will not be afraid," he said, his voice steady and sincere. "I want to thank both of you from the bottom of my heart. The way you both have fought for me is truly commendable. I don't know how I will ever be able to repay this favor of yours in this life."

His words touched me deeply, and I felt a surge of warmth and affection for him. "You don't need to repay us, Bhaskar," I replied softly. "We did it because we care about you. Seeing you happy and free is all the thanks we need."

As we sat there, sipping our coffee and sharing stories, the weight of the past seemed to lift, replaced by a sense of hope and possibility. The evening stretched on, filled with laughter and heartfelt conversations, and for the first time in a long while, Bhaskar's smile reached his eyes.

The café was filled with a warm, inviting ambiance as Bhaskar and I continued our conversation. I couldn't help but let a playful thought slip out, "By the way, to return the favor, you can marry me," I said to myself, feeling a rush of emotions. Controlling my feelings, I turned to Bhaskar and said, "Just become my dance partner in Didi's sangeet ceremony."

Bhaskar burst into laughter, his eyes twinkling with amusement. "Okay, I am ready," he replied, his laughter infectious.

Just then, the waiter approached our table. Before I could say anything, Bhaskar confidently placed our order. "One white sauce pasta and two fresh lime sodas, please. And could you bring me a pen?"

I raised an eyebrow, impressed by his newfound assertiveness. "Oho, impressive! You have changed, but it's nice to see you like this. And what is the pen for?" I asked, curiosity piqued.

Bhaskar smiled mysteriously, his eyes sparkling with a hint of mischief. "You'll see," he said, leaving me intrigued and excited for what was to come.

As we waited for our order, the anticipation of the sangeet ceremony and the promise of a dance together filled me with a sense of joy and hope. Whatever the future held, I knew that moments like these, filled with laughter and companionship, were the ones that truly mattered.

The waiter brought a pen, and Bhaskar immediately started writing something on the tissue paper kept on the table. "You will find out soon," he said with a playful smile, his eyes twinkling with mischief. I leaned in, trying to catch a glimpse of what he was writing, but he shielded the paper, keeping it a secret.

Finally, after what felt like an eternity, he finished writing and handed me the tissue paper. My heart raced with anticipation as I unfolded it. Written in Bhaskar's neat handwriting were the words:

To,
Niharika

"Time will pass,

Years will pass,

Many seasons will come and go,

You should remain like this because no one will come again like you,

I claim,

No matter how many eras will come and go".

From,
Bhaskar.

The sincerity and depth of his words touched my heart deeply. I looked up at Bhaskar, my emotions laid bare. "This is beautiful, Bhaskar," I whispered, my voice choked with emotion.

He smiled warmly, his eyes reflecting the same emotions. "You deserve every word, Niharika," he said softly.

In that moment, surrounded by the cozy ambiance of the café and the warmth of Bhaskar's presence, I felt an overwhelming sense of gratitude and love. Whatever the future held, I knew that with Bhaskar by my side, we could face anything together.

"Uh Bhaskar this is so cute," I said as I put the paper in my purse and kept it safely. "I will always keep it safe"

I wanted to say a lot after that but we both kept talking about useless things. There was only one thought going on in my mind but I kept a fake smile on my face and listened to him and replied to him with a smile. Then I felt that either he was really a fool or he had really lost his senses. Such a beautiful girl is sitting in front of him and has been trying to woo him for so long but he is just not able to understand. This continued for a long time and we both did not even realize that it was quite late. If I had not received Sarika Di's call, I would have probably sat there all night and kept listening to him.

"Do you know how to read time or have you forgotten that too in your love for Bhaskar? It is time for Mom and Dad to come. Anand and I are standing outside the cafe. Come quickly." Sarika Di told me on the call.

"Do you know what time it is? Come on, Didi and Jiju have come to pick me up." I told Bhaskar and then quickly left the cafe and sat in the back seat of Jiju's car.

We all sat quietly in the car like simple children and left for home "Congratulations, Bhaskar, finally you are free now" brother-in-law tried to start a conversation by saying this to Bhaskar but it was of no use. Bhaskar just smiled and said "Thank you, this would never have been possible without you all, so thank you from my heart" and when we reached home, we all started getting out of the car. While leaving I told Bhaskar "Come on time for practice tomorrow, I will tell you the time through message."

After coming home I started thinking about deciding the songs because I am a bit filmy, so I thought that songs would be the best way to make Bhaskar understand how much I love him. My mind was battling a storm whose beginning was unknown and where it would end was unknown, but I don't know why there was a small hope that this storm would take me to a better place.

The relationship of Shiv and Parvati is the most beautiful union for me in this world and I always wanted that whenever someone special comes into my life, my relationship with him should be an example for the world. While thinking this, my eyes left my mind, and I fell asleep dreaming of my union with Bhaskar.

Dreams indeed have a magical way of freeing our deepest desires and allowing us to live without the constraints of reality. As soon as I closed my eyes, I found myself ready to become Bhaskar's. In my dream, I took Bhaskar to the same hill where he used to visit the waterfall during his childhood and youth.

That day, in reality, I couldn't reach there, but dreams have no such limitations. Today, in the dream, we reached that waterfall, surrounded by the heavy rain. The sound of the cascading water mixed with the rhythmic patter of raindrops created a symphony that echoed through the lush greenery. The air was fresh and cool, filled with the scent of wet earth and blooming flowers.

Bhaskar and I stood there, drenched but exhilarated, the rain washing away all our fears and doubts. We laughed and danced, feeling the freedom that only dreams can offer. The waterfall, with its powerful yet soothing flow, seemed to cleanse our souls, leaving us with a sense of peace and unity.

In that dream, we were free to express our love without any reservations, and for a moment, it felt like the world was ours. The dream was a beautiful reminder of the possibilities that lay ahead, and as I woke up, I carried that sense of hope and freedom with me, ready to face whatever the future held.

I was wearing a white saree, dreams, so anything is possible, please don't think about what I am saying, and Bhaskar was wearing a white shirt, we both got very wet in the rain. But we were not worried because the one who is in the fever of love does not worry about any other fever

I ran and stood under the waterfall. Bhaskar also came running after me and took me in his arms. Forgetting everything we just stood on that deserted hill embracing each other, unconscious. Bhaskar's grip was slowly getting stronger and my grip was getting weaker. He was trying to forget everything and embrace me within him and I was surrendering myself to him to get wrapped up within him.

The winds were now changing their direction and my body was shivering in the strong winds. Every part of my body was now dependent on the warmth of Bhaskar's body. Sometimes his hands touched my thin waist and sometimes my chest and I would become happy just by feeling the warmth of his hands and that loving touch, as if God has touched a devotee

As the speed of the wind increased, the rhythm of Bhaskar's hands and the beat of my heart synchronized, creating a symphony of emotions. Each touch of his hand felt like a divine blessing, purifying my soul and drawing me deeper into his devotion. His caresses were gentle yet powerful, making me feel cherished and adored as if he were a god bestowing his love upon me.

My body, once tense and rigid, began to relax under his touch. The warmth of his body was the only thing keeping me alive, a beacon of heat in the cold wind. Bhaskar's lips found their way to my forehead, planting a tender kiss that sent shivers down my spine. Slowly, he moved towards my neck, his breath warm against my skin.

With a delicate touch, Bhaskar brushed the wet strands of hair away from my face, tucking them behind my ears. His fingers lingered for a moment, sending a thrill through me. Then, his lips met mine, and it felt as if he had breathed his very soul into me. The connection was electric, igniting a fire within me that burned away all hesitation.

At that moment, my madness knew no bounds. I wanted to break free from all constraints and surrender completely to Bhaskar, to embrace the love that was blossoming between us. The world around us faded into oblivion, leaving only the two of us, entwined in a dance of passion and devotion.

As Bhaskar's lips lingered on mine, the world around us seemed to dissolve, leaving only the warmth of his embrace and the intensity of our connection. The wind howled outside, but within the cocoon of our shared moment, there was only peace and a growing sense of belonging.

Bhaskar pulled back slightly, his eyes searching mine for any sign of hesitation. Finding none, he smiled—a smile that spoke of understanding, acceptance, and a deep, abiding love. "Niharika," he whispered, his voice a soothing balm to my racing heart, "you are my light in the darkness."

His words wrapped around me like a warm blanket, and I felt a surge of emotion that threatened to overwhelm me. "Bhaskar," I replied, my voice trembling with the weight of my feelings, "I never knew love could be like this. So pure, so consuming."

He gently cupped my face in his hands, his thumbs brushing away the tears that had begun to fall. "We have both been through so much," he said softly, "but together, we can heal. Together, we can find happiness."

I nodded, unable to speak as the depth of his words sank in. Bhaskar's love was a beacon, guiding me through the storm of my past and into a future filled with hope and promise.

As we stood there, wrapped in each other's arms, I knew that this was just the beginning of our journey. There would be challenges ahead, but with Bhaskar by my side, I felt ready to face anything. Our love was a sanctuary, a place where we could both find solace and strength.

The wind outside began to die down as if acknowledging the calm that had settled between us. Bhaskar took my hand, leading me towards the warmth of the fireplace. We sat down together, the flickering flames casting a soft glow on our faces.

"Tell me about your dreams, Niharika," Bhaskar said, his voice filled with genuine curiosity. "What do you see for our future?"

I smiled, feeling a sense of excitement bubble up inside me. "I see us building a life together," I began, "a life filled with love, laughter, and endless adventures. I see us supporting each other, growing together, and creating a home where we both feel safe and cherished."

Bhaskar's eyes sparkled with joy as he listened. "And I see us traveling the world," he added, "exploring new places, meeting new people, and making memories that will last a lifetime."

With the alarm bell, Bhaskar left me and I returned from the world of dreams to reality where I had a mountain of problems in front of me and the burden of bringing the truth in front of the world and Bhaskar.

144

CHAPTER SEVEN

I Love You

I had a feeling that something special was going to happen as soon as I woke up. The remnants of Bhaskar's dream still lingered in my mind, a sweet echo of the night. By the time I emerged from my reverie, my mom and dad had already reached my aunt's house. As I opened my eyes, my dad's voice reached my ears, grounding me back to reality.

"Get up, Niharika! How long will you sleep?" My father's voice broke through my dreams. He was a doctor by profession, but his youthful spirit made him seem more like a 20-year-old. He never treated me like a daughter; instead, he always considered me his friend. And I, in turn, never saw him as just my father but as my closest confidant.

There were times I felt like sharing everything with Daddy, but this was not a small matter. I couldn't just drop such a bombshell on him. So, when I heard his voice, I groaned and replied, "You don't let me sleep in at home, and now you've come here to wake me up too?"

"Anyway, I hurried down to meet him, my heart pounding with anticipation. Before I could utter a single word, he stunned me by asking, 'Who is Bhaskar? Introduce him to me."

"With a mix of curiosity and surprise, I asked, 'Who told you about Bhaskar, and what did he say?"

"Daddy replied, 'You were the one who told me that day when we talked on the phone."

I breathed a sigh of relief when he said, "Oh, okay, yes, I remember. Yes, I will introduce you. What's the hurry? He will come today to practice dance for Di's sangeet. I'm dancing with him; he's my dance partner." I then went upstairs to Di's room, saying, "I'll come back after getting ready."

Di, who was also sitting there, looked equally shocked. She quickly followed me and exclaimed, "When was this decided? You're not planning to cause any scandal at my wedding, right?"

"Oh no, Didi, I just want to dance," I reassured her. "Suggest a song that I can dance to with Bhaskar, one that will also let me express what's in my heart." I said this and then started laughing shyly.

Didi and I sat down to brainstorm. It wasn't long before the doorbell rang, and to our surprise, Divyasha arrived with Bhaskar.

Aunty opened the door and warmly hugged Divyasha, saying, "Come, my love. I am so happy to see you this joyful." Then, turning to Bhaskar, she added, "Bhaisahab, please come in and sit. Divyasha, bring Papa inside. Divyasha visits us often, but this is your first time here. This girl has become close to all our family members. You have a very sweet daughter."

Then she called out to Sarika Didi, "Sarika, Divyasha and Bhaisahab are here. Come down and join us!"

"Bhaskar has arrived. I hope he doesn't say anything to Papa after meeting him," I thought nervously. Saying this, I dashed downstairs. Just as I was about to bring them both to the upstairs room, Papa emerged from his room.

But who can avoid destiny? Papa emerged from his room and greeted, "Namaste, Bhaisahab. I've heard so much about you from my daughter. I've been eager to meet you, and now here you are. I was just about to take a bath when Nirmala called out to me. As soon as I heard you had arrived, I rushed out to see you." With that, Papa moved forward to greet Bhaskar.

I quickly grabbed Divyasha's hand and hurriedly led both of them upstairs, calling back to Papa, "You can meet him later. Right now, we have to prepare for the dance."

Bhaskar, Sarika Di, Divyasha, and I sat down to discuss the songs. Divyasha mentioned, "Bhaskar is a huge fan of Hrithik Roshan and used to dance to all his songs. Grandma told me that 'Aap Mujhe Achche Lagne Lage' was his favorite."

"Done, then 'Aap Mujhe Achche Lagne Lage,' Bhaskar," I declared. After saying this, I paused for a moment. Sarika Di, sitting nearby, pinched my hand, snapping me back to reality. Trying to cover up the awkward silence, I quickly added, "Let's prepare for the dance. Will that work?"

Bhaskar didn't say a word; he simply raised his thumb and nodded in agreement.

Divyasha and Sarika Di had already planned everything, so we decided to meet in the evening on the terrace of Sarika Di's house. Di's other friends and a couple of our siblings were also going to join us by evening.

As Bhaskar and Divyasha were about to leave, I grabbed Divyasha's hand. While Bhaskar was descending the stairs, I whispered to her, "Keep Bhaskar away from Papa. If he starts talking about our meetings in detail, it could turn into a mess."

Caught up in the moment, I blurted out to Bhaskar once more, "Aap Mujhe Achche Lagne Lage." Then, with a thumbs-up, I added, "Nice song."

Both of them left for home, but Bhaskar's cold reaction left me feeling disheartened. Sensing my mood, Sarika Di tried to cheer me up, saying, "Niharika, this isn't going to be easy. Brace yourself. You'll have to work hard to win Bhaskar over."

I spent the entire day with headphones in my ears, listening to music and practicing dance steps. I was determined to impress Bhaskar when he arrived.

Sarika Di suggested that I call Bhaskar a little earlier so we could spend some time alone before everyone else arrived. This was exactly what I wanted, so I called Bhaskar and asked him to come early. We reached the roof about an hour before everyone else was due. Since the roofs of his house and Sarika Di's house were connected, he came directly from his roof.

As soon as he stepped onto the terrace, I couldn't help but say once more, "Aap Mujhe Achche Lagne Lage."

"Did you like the song?" Bhaskar asked me.

I wanted to say that I wasn't sure about the song, but I was definitely starting to like him. Instead, I said, "Yes, it's a very good song. I must say there's so much truth in it that it touched my heart," while carefully hiding my true feelings.

"Great, so how do we start?" Bhaskar asked me.

"You'll walk from the left corner of the stage to the center while I stand at the right corner, watching you. Then, you'll turn around, and I'll stand behind you with my back to you. We'll both simultaneously raise our hands to our waists and turn to face each other." Bhaskar interrupted me, saying, "I liked Hrithik Roshan, but I'm not Hrithik Roshan. I didn't quite get that. Can you explain it again?"

I took his hand and guided him to the left corner, demonstrating how he should walk to the center of the stage. I explained the entire dance to him step by step. After a couple of rehearsals, he got the hang of it. We practiced the whole dance two more times, but he was just going through the motions. It felt like he had locked all his emotions away in a trunk at home.

I thought to myself, "What an idiot! A beautiful young girl is dancing so closely, and he feels nothing." Out loud, I told him, "You have to work very hard." He responded, "This time I did all the steps correctly." Internally, I sighed, "I'm not talking about the dance; I'm talking about impressing you." Hiding my true feelings, I said, "Where have your feelings gone?"

"Maybe I've buried all my feelings after enduring so much for so many years. I'm sorry. I hope your dance doesn't get ruined because of me. You should find another partner; there's still time," he said to me.

"Now, neither time nor emotions are in my control. You'll have to do something," I said, then turned away and played the song.

I had lost my senses by now. After playing the song, I approached Bhaskar, my heart pounding in my chest. Holding his shoulders, I leaned in close, my breath warm against his ear as I whispered, "AAP MUJHEY ACHAEY LAGNEY LAGEY." His eyes widened with a mix of surprise and longing. He gently placed his hand on my waist, pulling me closer as we began to dance again.

This time, there was an undeniable yearning in his eyes, a desire that had been suppressed for so many years. Our movements became more fluid, more intimate, as if we were the only two people in the world. The dance was sensual, our bodies moving in perfect harmony, and I could feel the heat rising between us.

We had just completed half the dance when the intensity became too much to bear. Both of us were on the brink of losing control. I was already drowning in the emotions, but for Bhaskar, this was a new and overwhelming sensation. He abruptly stopped the song, his voice trembling as he said, "I can't do this anymore, let's take a break."

After Bhaskar stepped aside, the crowd quickly gathered around us, leaving no room for us to continue our practice. The moment was lost in the hustle and bustle, and soon we found ourselves heading back home.

The next day was my sister's sangeet ceremony, and the house was a whirlwind of activity. I was caught up in a flurry of tasks, from decorating to coordinating with relatives. The wedding preparations consumed every minute of my day, leaving no time to talk to Bhaskar or practice our dance again.

The anticipation and unspoken words hung in the air, but amidst the chaos of the wedding house, there was simply no opportunity to reconnect. The day passed in a blur, filled with laughter, music, and the vibrant energy of the sangeet, but that moment with Bhaskar remained unfinished, a lingering thought in the back of my mind.

We met directly at Sarika Di's sangeet ceremony. The thought of performing in front of my parents and the entire family made my nerves jittery. To muster up some courage, I downed a whole bottle of beer. The alcohol coursed through my veins, giving me a false sense of boldness.

As Bhaskar and I stood backstage, waiting for our cue, I turned to him, my vision slightly blurred and my words slurred. "Forget whatever has happened till date," I said, my voice tinged with the intoxication of beer. "Just for once, consider me the one whom you wanted, the one with whom you had dreamt of love."

His eyes widened in surprise, and for a moment, the world seemed to stand still. The noise of the crowd faded into the background, and it was just the two of us, standing on the precipice of something new and unspoken.

Bhaskar remained silent, his expression unreadable. It was time for our performance. As we stepped onto the stage together, the entire crowd turned their attention to us. My heart pounded like a fast train, each beat echoing in my ears.

The music began, and we started dancing. Every move felt electrified, the energy between us palpable. The audience faded into the background as we lost ourselves in the rhythm. The dance was a blend of passion and precision, each step bringing us closer, both physically and emotionally.

Despite the nerves and the alcohol, there was a connection, a silent understanding that this moment was special. The crowd watched in awe, but for us, it was as if we were the only two people in the room, sharing a dance that spoke volumes more than words ever could.

It sounds like the dance was a transformative moment for both of us. The combination of my feelings for

Bhaskar and the effects of the beer created an intense, almost magical experience. As I danced, it was as if the music itself was guiding my movements, weaving a spell around us both.

Bhaskar's touch on my waist felt electrifying, sending waves of heat through my body. Each glance into his eyes deepened the connection, making it feel as though we were no longer two separate individuals, but one entity moving in perfect harmony. The world around us faded away, leaving just the two of us, lost in the dance and the emotions it stirred.

It seems like Bhaskar was equally caught up in the moment, his silence and actions speaking louder than words. The dance allowed both of us to express feelings that had been building up, creating a beautiful, unforgettable experience.

The dance ended, and the entire crowd erupted into applause, their cheers filling the room. It was clear that no one had ever seen such a performance before. We bowed to everyone, our hearts still racing from the intensity of the moment.

As we stepped down from the stage, Bhaskar gave me a gentle hug, his embrace warm and reassuring. He then flashed a double thumbs-up, his eyes sparkling with pride and something deeper. Without a word, he went and sat in the crowd, leaving me to process the whirlwind of emotions.

The applause continued, but all I could think about was the connection we had shared during the dance.

It was a moment that would stay with me forever, a beautiful blend of passion, courage, and unspoken feelings.

I stood there backstage, speechless and overwhelmed by a sense of finality. It felt as if everything was coming to an end, and the thought of never seeing Bhaskar again after tonight weighed heavily on my heart. The intensity of the moment, combined with the fear of losing him, was too much to bear.

In a desperate attempt to numb the emotions swirling inside me, I quickly ran towards the room and grabbed two bottles of beer. Without thinking, I drank them both, hoping to drown the sorrow and uncertainty that threatened to consume me. The alcohol burned as it went down, but it was nothing compared to the ache in my chest.

As the room started to spin, I couldn't help but wonder what the future held for Bhaskar and me. The night had been magical, but reality was beginning to set in, and I was left grappling with the fear of what might come next.

After drinking the beer, I felt a surge of boldness. I went straight to the stage where Di was standing and whispered in her ear, "Sorry Di." Without waiting for her reaction, I climbed up on the stage and took the mic from the anchor, who was just about to end the sangeet ceremony.

"There's still one surprise left!" I announced, my voice echoing through the hall. The crowd turned their attention to me, curiosity and excitement in their eyes.

The music started, and I began dancing to "Zara Zara Behta Hai Mehekta Hai Aaj To Mera Tan Badan." The melody flowed through me, and I let the emotions of the night guide my movements. Each step was filled with passion and longing, a final expression of everything I felt.

The audience watched in awe, and for a moment, it felt like I was dancing not just for them, but for Bhaskar, for myself, and for the love that had blossomed in the most unexpected way.

I got down from the stage and made my way through the audience, my heart pounding with every step. Bhaskar was sitting with my father, and as I approached, I felt a surge of determination. I took Bhaskar's hand in mine, feeling the warmth of his touch, and looked deeply into his eyes.

"Bhaskar Sharma," I began, my voice steady but filled with emotion, "I love you. I fell in love with you from the day I saw you for the first time. Since then, I have tried to stop myself from loving you many times, but each time I did, I found myself falling for you even more. Now, I can no longer hold back. If Niharika Sharma is to belong to anyone, if she is to give her body and soul to anyone, it will be only you. I love you with all my heart and soul, and I have no shame in saying that I have already given myself to you in my heart."

The room seemed to hold its breath, the weight of my words hanging in the air. It was a moment of pure vulnerability and truth, and I could see the impact it had on Bhaskar as he looked back at me, his eyes filled with a mix of surprise, emotion, and something deeper.

Bhaskar stood there, listening to every word like a statue, his eyes locked onto mine. I could see the conflict in his gaze—part of him seemed to want to pull away, to escape the intensity of the moment, but something deeper held him in place. Perhaps he wanted to hug me, to tell me that he felt the same way, but was struggling to find the words.

I didn't know what would happen next, but I knew I had to let him know everything in my heart. I tightened my grip on his hands, feeling the warmth and strength in his touch, and let the tide of my emotions flow freely.

"Bhaskar," I continued, my voice steady but filled with emotion, "I needed to tell you this. Whatever happens next, I had to let you know how I feel. You mean the world to me, and I couldn't keep it inside any longer."

The room seemed to fade away, leaving just the two of us in that moment of raw honesty. I waited, my heart pounding, to see how he would respond.

"If you wish to refuse today, then of course you can refuse, but remember that whenever you need someone close to you, Niharika Sharma will be there for you. I have fallen in love with you to such an extent that now no one else can come into my life except you. I will not let anyone else come into my life. If you are there, then I am there. My happiness is in your happiness. If you don't make me yours, then I will breathe but won't be alive."

Tears streamed down my face as I sat on the ground in front of him, my emotions overwhelming me. With a voice choked with sobs, I screamed, "Bhaskar, I love you, will you marry me?"

The room fell silent, the weight of my words hanging in the air. Bhaskar's eyes were filled with a mix of emotions, and for a moment, time seemed to stand still. The crowd watched in stunned silence, waiting for his response.

Seeing me cry, it was as if even the heavens couldn't hold back their tears. Suddenly, the sky opened up, and rain poured down with such intensity that it felt like a cloud had burst right above us. The crowd scattered, seeking shelter from the deluge, but I remained where I was, sitting on the ground, my eyes locked onto Bhaskar's.

He stood there, drenched, listening to my every word, his gaze never leaving mine. The rain soaked us both, but it felt like we were in our own world, suspended in that moment. I waited, hoping for a response, but he just stood there, silent and unmoving.

Then, my father came and gently took my hand, pulling me away from Bhaskar. As I was led away, my eyes never left his. He stood there, getting drenched in the rain, watching me go, and I could see the turmoil in his eyes. It was a moment of raw emotion, one that neither of us would forget.

Papa pulled me away and brought me home, where all the relatives had gathered. The atmosphere was tense, with Mummy, Aunt, and everyone else crying as if my declaration of love had sparked a world war and the world was about to end. The weight of their reactions made the situation feel even more overwhelming.

As I went upstairs with Sarika Di, the hurtful comments from my relatives echoed from downstairs. It felt like each word was a dagger, piercing through the haze of my emotions. But then, I heard Papa's voice rise above the murmurs, calm and resolute.

"She is my daughter, and she will never do anything that will embarrass me. So I will see what to do next. You all go and take some rest. Please forgive me if my daughter has caused any disturbance in the function."

Papa, trying to restore some order, told Sarika Di to take me to her room. She gently guided me upstairs, helped me change out of my wet clothes, and tucked me into bed. The exhaustion from the emotional rollercoaster and the effects of the beer began to take their toll, and I felt myself drifting off to sleep, my mind still replaying the events of the night.

His words were a balm to my wounded heart. Despite everything, Papa stood up for me, his unwavering support shining through. I felt a surge of gratitude and love for him, wishing I could go down and kiss his forehead to show my appreciation. But the exhaustion and the effects of the beer were too much, and I soon fell into a deep sleep, comforted by the knowledge that Papa was on my side.

As I lay there, I couldn't help but wonder what Bhaskar was thinking and what the future held for us. The night had been a whirlwind of emotions, and now, all I could do was wait and see what tomorrow would bring.

The next morning, Papa gently woke me up with a glass of lemon water. As I sipped it, he sat beside me, his eyes filled with concern and curiosity. I avoided his gaze, feeling the weight of the previous night's events.

After a moment of silence, Papa finally spoke. "Did what happened yesterday happen because of intoxication, or did you say every word to Bhaskar from your heart? And does Bhaskar feel the same for you? Whatever you said yesterday in intoxication, will you be able to say all that to Bhaskar without intoxication in front of the whole world? If you have even one percent fear in your heart, then tell me right now."

His questions hung in the air, each one piercing through the fog of my mind. I knew I had to be honest with him, and more importantly, with myself. The love I felt for Bhaskar was real, and I needed to find the courage to stand by my words, no matter the circumstances.

"Papa, whatever I said last night, I said every word from my heart. I truly love Bhaskar, and now I will not be able to love anyone else except him. I am not afraid of society, but I am deeply affected by your and Mummy's feelings. I love both of you as much as I love Bhaskar. So now that you know everything, if you say that I cannot be with Bhaskar, then I promise I will not marry him. But it is also true that I will never marry anyone else because I can suppress my desires for your happiness, but not my love. I will love Bhaskar till my last breath, whether I am with him or away from him."

As I spoke, tears began to flow from my eyes. Papa listened intently, his expression softening with each word. The room was filled with a heavy silence, the weight of my confession hanging in the air. I waited, my heart pounding, for his response.

"Does Bhaskar have the same feelings for you?" Papa asked, his voice gentle but probing.

"I don't know, Papa," I admitted, my voice trembling slightly. "Because before today, I have never told him my feelings. But Bhaskar's daughter, Divyasha, knows everything, and she wants the same thing. She has no objection."

"Can you give me Divyasha's number?" Papa asked, his tone gentle but serious.

I forwarded Divyasha's number from my phone, trusting that whatever Papa did would be for the best. As he called Divyasha and left the room, my mind raced with thoughts of what might happen next. Would Papa talk to Bhaskar? Would Bhaskar reach out to Papa? The uncertainty gnawed at me, and I couldn't help but worry about the potential consequences.

What if Bhaskar went back into trauma because of my actions? The thought was unbearable, and I knew I would never forgive myself if that happened. I felt a deep sense of helplessness, and in that moment, I turned to my faith.

"Oh my Shiv," I whispered, "only you can unite me and Bhaskar now."

I closed my eyes, hoping for a sign, a miracle that would bring clarity and peace to this tumultuous situation. All I could do was wait and trust that everything would unfold as it was meant to.

It must have been around two in the afternoon when Papa called me and invited me to Bhaskar's house. I got up immediately, still in the same clothes, and rushed over. The atmosphere there felt tense and a bit strange. Bhaskar and Papa were sitting across from each other, and Divyasha was sitting quietly in the corner. My heart was pounding, filled with anxiety and hope that everything would be alright.

As I entered, Papa looked at me and said, "Come and sit here." He stood up from his seat in front of Bhaskar and moved to sit next to him, gesturing for me to take the seat opposite Bhaskar.

I walked over, my legs feeling like they might give out at any moment, and sat down. The room was filled with a heavy silence, and I could feel the weight of everyone's eyes on me. I took a deep breath, trying to steady my nerves, and looked up to meet Bhaskar's gaze, waiting for what would come next.

"Do you love Bhaskar?" Papa asked, his eyes shifting between Bhaskar and me.

I took a deep breath, feeling the weight of the moment. "Yes, Papa," I said, my voice steady but filled with emotion. "I love Bhaskar with all my heart. I have loved him from the moment I first saw him, and that love has only grown stronger over time."

I glanced at Bhaskar, hoping to see some sign of his feelings. The room was silent, everyone waiting for what would come next. My heart pounded in my chest, but I knew I had to be honest and true to my feelings, no matter what the outcome might be.

Bhaskar got up from the sofa after hearing my confession and walked straight to the drawing-room window, staring out in silence. My heart raced as I looked at my father, who gave me a reassuring nod, signaling me to go to Bhaskar.

I stood up, my hands folded nervously, and walked over to where Bhaskar was standing. The room felt heavy with anticipation. I stood beside him, close enough to feel his presence but not touching, waiting for him to say something, anything.

"Bhaskar," I began softly, my voice trembling slightly, "I meant every word I said. I love you, and I need to know how you feel. Please, talk to me."

The silence stretched on, and I could feel the weight of the moment pressing down on us both. I hoped that he would open up, that he would share his feelings and give us a chance to move forward together.

Bhaskar looked deeply into Niharika's eyes, his voice gentle yet firm. "Niharika," he began, "you are an incredibly wonderful girl, but what you believe to be love is merely an infatuation. Let go of your stubbornness. Embrace the joy of Sarika's wedding, return to Delhi, focus on your studies, build a bright future, establish your career, and then find a truly good man to marry and fall in love with."

"I am an old man compared to you," Bhaskar began, but I interrupted him, my voice unwavering. "Bhaskar, my career, my future, my love—everything is tied to you. This is neither mere attraction nor stubbornness. I may not know much about love, but I do know this: I will either be yours or no one else's. If you don't consider me yours today, it doesn't matter. I will stay in this city, complete my studies, become someone, and wait for you until my last breath."

Papa and Divyasha stood there, their eyes fixed on us as we stood our ground, each trying to convince the other. Neither of us wavered; Bhaskar remained steadfast in his stance, and so did I. The conclusion seemed elusive. Frustrated by our stalemate, Papa and Divyasha stepped in to mediate. Divyasha gently guided her father to one side, while Papa took my arm and led me to the other.

Nothing had changed; the tension hung in the air. Papa took Divyasha's hand and led her aside, whispering something in her ear before returning to me. "Let's go now," he said softly. Meanwhile, Bhaskar stood by the window, staring out without blinking, lost in his thoughts. I grasped Papa's hand, and together we left Bhaskar's house, the weight of unspoken words lingering behind us.

"I am proud of you, Niharika. You have truly shown that you are my daughter," Papa said, his voice filled with pride. "I am very happy today, and I promise you will marry Bhaskar. If I cannot make this happen, I will never force you to marry anyone else unless you wish to or find someone yourself." Hearing these words, my happiness knew no bounds. I ran to Sarika Di's house, my heart soaring, and hugged her tightly.

Papa left me at Sarika Di's house and then headed back towards Bhaskar's place. Meanwhile, Divyasha gathered some belongings into a polybag, and the two of them rode off together on her scooter, disappearing down the street.

Evening had fallen, and Papa was still nowhere to be seen. Just as I was about to call him, he walked into Sarika Di's room, holding a wedding dress. "I am proud of you, my daughter," he said, his voice filled with emotion. "I had many dreams about your wedding, but I have no regrets because what you are doing is greater than my dreams. I admire your determination and your passion for love. Tomorrow, it's your wedding too, alongside Sarika's. Get ready."

"Is Bhaskar ready?" I asked, my voice trembling with anticipation.

"It has to happen. You just get ready," Papa replied firmly before turning and walking away.

Respect

Papa's words had kindled a spark of hope within me, but I remained restless. Bhaskar was still entangled in the memories of his past relationship. If only I had more time, I could have shown him the depth of my love. As the clock's hands moved, not only was time slipping away, but so was my hope. With Di's wedding set for tomorrow, I sat alone in her room, feeling isolated and helpless. I longed for Bhaskar to come, to hold me in his arms, and to whisper, "I love you, Niharika."

Night was approaching, and after the evening function, Mom entered Sarika Di's room. "Niharika, why are you sitting here alone like this?" she asked gently. "Sarika has called you so many times, and I have too. Why aren't you answering your phone?" Her voice was calm and filled with love.

This was the first time I was speaking to my mother since the incident at the sangeet function. I had expected her to be angry or upset, but as I looked at her expressions, it felt like I was dreaming. Her calm and loving demeanor was a stark contrast to what I had imagined.

"Mummy, you're not angry with me? What I did yesterday was beyond my control," I said softly, my voice barely above a whisper.

"Love is a powerful force, my daughter. When it strikes, it can bewilder even the wisest of people. Why should I be angry about it?" Mummy said, her voice filled with understanding. "I am proud that when my daughter fell in love, she did so openly and honestly." She came and sat beside me, her presence comforting.

I rested my head on Mummy's lap and asked, "Mummy, have I done something wrong? Bhaskar is so much older than me and..."

Mummy interrupted me gently, "Love has nothing to do with age, my daughter. Love is about emotions and respect. Your father has already told me how deeply you love and respect Bhaskar ji."

After gently caressing my head for a while, my mother spoke softly, "The foundation of any relationship is respect. Love endures only as long as we continue to respect each other."

"Is talking with love and bowing your head to accept what the other person says, respecting them, Mom?" I asked, my voice filled with curiosity.

"No, respect is a feeling that transcends words," Mummy explained. "It's not about bowing your head or blindly accepting what someone says. True respect is found in the eyes and the heart, and it cannot be faked. That's why you must always respect yourself, Bhaskar ji, and your love for him."

"Bitch! Have you come here for my wedding or to sulk in your room?" Sarika Di stormed towards me, her lehenga swishing furiously around her ankles. Her eyes blazed with anger as she confronted my mother, "Aunty, you can talk to your daughter later. Right now, I need to teach her a lesson."

"Whatever pleases you," she said, gently lifting my head from her lap. As she stood up to leave, she turned back and added, "I'm leaving, Niharika. Always remember to respect your love. If not today, then tomorrow, Bhaskar ji will have to come."

As soon as Mummy left, Sarika Di pulled me into a tight hug. "Niharika," she whispered urgently, "do you know what all these relatives are saying about you?"

"Yes, sister, that's exactly why I'm hiding in your room," I confessed, my voice barely above a whisper.

"Why are you hiding? You haven't done anything wrong," Sarika Di reassured me, her voice filled with warmth. "I'm with you, and so are Mummy, Papa, Aunty, and Uncle. And guess what? Anand and his parents sent their best wishes when they heard your story."

"And Bhaskar?" I asked, my voice trembling slightly.

"He will have to agree. If he doesn't, I'll scold him and drag him to you myself. After all, it's a question of my sister's love," Sarika Di declared with determination. She then walked over to the wardrobe, pulling out a beautiful suit. Handing it to me, she said, "Go and get ready quickly."

I got ready for Di's happiness, even though my heart wasn't in it. She took my hand and led me to the terrace. "Di, why are we going to the terrace?" I asked, puzzled. She just smiled and said, "Keep walking quietly." As we reached the top, she crossed her fingers and whispered, "I hope everything goes well today."

As we made our way to the terrace, my mind was racing. Today is my sister's wedding, such a monumental day for her, yet she's thinking so much about me. And here I am, feeling like I've done everything to ruin her special day. Lost in these thoughts, we finally reached the terrace.

"Sister, now tell me what happened. Why have we come to the roof?" I demanded, my curiosity getting the better of me.

"You will know it soon," Didi said mysteriously, pointing ahead with her finger. "Look over there."

In front of me, Divyasha stood on the roof with Bhaskar. Just as I had no idea what was going to happen up here, Bhaskar was equally unaware that he would meet me on the roof.

Divyasha turned to Bhaskar, and Sarika Di looked at me, both speaking in unison, "Whatever happens between you two, talk as little as possible and leave it on a good note so that neither your life nor anyone else's is affected." With that, they left us alone on the terrace.

Bhaskar was exuding a sense of maturity as he took the first step towards me. I responded by taking the second step, my eyes fixed on him, filled with hope that today he would finally accept my love.

"Niharika," Bhaskar called out to me with tenderness.

"Bhaskar," I responded.

There were so many unspoken thoughts swirling in our minds, so many questions left unanswered. Summoning all my courage, I finally spoke up, "Do you have a cigarette?"

He reached into his pocket, offering me the packet, and said, "Why are you doing this to yourself? Please don't do this."

I anticipated his response, so I wordlessly placed the cigarette in my mouth and said, "Give me the lighter too."

He quickly retrieved the lighter and lit my cigarette. As he reached for a cigarette for himself, I stopped his hand and declared, "You can decide about life, but I have made my decision about cigarettes. We'll share it."

After taking a couple of puffs, I handed him the cigarette and remarked, "Raindrops are so fortunate. They fall to the ground and become one. No one questions which cloud they came from, or whether they are big or small. They are simply one drop for all of us. When they descend from the sky, they are separate, but on the ground, they become one."

"Niharika," Bhaskar said.

"Yes, tell me Bhaskar," I responded.

"Each drop has a different destiny which is pre-decided. Yes, they become one as soon as they fall on the earth, but they also get separated as they go further along the flow," Bhaskar added, elaborating on my point.

"What if God has decided the same destination for those two drops?" I countered.

Bhaskar fell silent, unable to respond. After a moment of contemplation, he spoke in a firm tone, "Niharika, don't mistake the sympathy in your heart for love."

"My love is genuine, Bhaskar. It holds nothing but love and respect for you," I insisted.

"How much do you really know about me? What if Aisha was right and I was wrong?" Bhaskar began, but I interrupted him, placing my hand over his mouth. "This evening belongs only to us. Don't let anyone, especially Aisha, come between us."

"In a little while, all my relatives will gather, and after Di's wedding, I will probably return to Delhi. Whether you accept me today or not is your choice, but I will continue to visit Ajmer every year, hoping that one day you will see the truth of my love," I declared.

"Maybe we should leave now," Bhaskar suggested.

"If you want to go, you can. I won't stop you. But if my love is true, you will come back to me," I asserted.

Bhaskar remained silent, and we both sat quietly for some time, trying to understand each other's silence. After about two minutes, Bhaskar finally spoke, "I've been experiencing back pain for the last two years."

"I will massage your back and apply balm everyday" I said.

"My hair has also turned grey now, and I don't prefer to dye it," said Bhaskar.

"I also don't like dyed hair. Don't ever do it" I said.

"The way I have smoked without caring about my health, I might get cancer in a few years," Bhaskar said.

"I also smoke and anyway why should I think about something that hasn't happened yet, that is a matter for later, I don't think that far ahead" I said.

Bhaskar's eyes had become wet. He was probably trying to free his emotions from the shackles of age. He touched me for the first time today. He held me by the shoulders and said, "Then think about the future, Niharika please think about yourself."

I just wanted to surrender myself to Bhaskar, when he held me by the shoulders, I surrendered myself to him. "Bhaskar, Aap mujhey achey lagney lagey."

"Niharika, this is real life, not a movie where you get emotional and take some wrong steps and regret it later, so come to your senses and go back to your world of happiness and fun, I may not be able to give you anything except tears in your entire life" Bhaskar told me.

"It is only in real life that emotions are truly recognized, Bhaskar. My happiness lies in being with you, I enjoy when you call out my name. You are right that this is not a movie where there is a hero and a heroine, this is the story of you and me which God himself is directing" I told Bhaskar.

Bhaskar hugged me tightly and I also held him tightly, then he gently pushed me away and said, "I am going to Rishikesh tonight, probably I will stay there from now on, you take care of yourself and please move forward in your life, all this love is nonsense, don't ruin your life by getting drowned in this useless talk, please go now" and went away from there.

I waited for him and stood there in a corner of the roof for a long time. Then after some time when Sarika Di and Divyasha came, I hugged them and started crying loudly. Both of them held me and brought me back to the room. Then Sarika Di asked me "What happened?"

"Bhaskar is leaving Didi, Bhaskar is leaving Divyasha, please stop him, I will go or not come back in his life if this is what he wants but I will not be able to bear any pain he faces because of me" I said and got up and went to the bathroom to hide the failure of my love.

All the relatives had arrived in the evening, and we all had also reached the venue, everyone was allotted their rooms, so I too went to my room and got ready by wearing the wedding dress and started waiting for Bhaskar. It was night but I had not turned on the lights of my room. I wanted to drown myself in the darkness because without Bhaskar there was only darkness left in my life.

Time was passing and with every second my dream of living with Bhaskar was getting weaker. Now only Bhole Baba was the one who could give a name to this relationship. I remembered my deity Mahadev with all my might and said "I have lost Mahadev, I have lost Bhaskar forever"

I was looking out of the window in the hope that Bhaskar would return. Bhaskar did not come but a storm came and the glass of the window broke and scattered on the ground. I was looking at the scattered glass and wondering if my life would also be shattered in this storm.

Time was passing by and there was silence in the entire venue but suddenly the sound of drums and band music reached my ears and the firecrackers touching the sky lit up my dark room.

After some time when Sarika Di came to pick me up, she said, "I am impressed by the power of your love" Then she saluted me and said, "Come Bhaskar is waiting for you downstairs."

As soon as I heard this, I rushed to the wedding venue the sound of my anklets was echoing in the entire corridor and the victory flag of my love was waving with screams. Bhaskar was standing in front of me and I ran and hugged him tightly. My happiness knew no bounds. Tears were not stopping from flowing from my eyes. No, these were not tears of sorrow. These were tears of love, of the dream of happiness being fulfilled.

Bhaskar took me in his arms and the heavy rain along with strong winds started dancing on this union of ours. We both stood for a long time embracing each other without saying anything.

My father put his hand on my head and while consoling me said, "Niharika, today you have explained the true meaning of love to the world. If not today, then tomorrow the whole world will appreciate your and Bhaskar's love story."

Papa took us both by the hand and led us to the wedding altar and Pandit ji started reciting the mantras and finally, the time came when Bhaskar was about to fill sindoor in my parting and make me wear mangalsutra, before he could fill my parting, I stopped him and said, "I love you, do you love me?"

"Niharika, yes I love you, and more than that I respect you. You have given a new definition of love. For some, love can be physical and for some, it can be connected to emotions. But your love gives respect to a person and it makes you different from the world. Love comes into everyone's life and maybe with time that love May or may not end but respect always stays in heart. If respect ends, then neither loves remains nor the person.

The respect you gave me ended my trauma; it is your respect that forced me to understand that your love is enough. My age has nothing to do with our love." After saying this, Bhaskar sat down on his knees and said, "Niharika Sharma, will you marry me? I don't know how much of my life is left but whatever life is left, I want to live it happily with you. Will you promise to give me that life?"

I picked Bhaskar up and said "Yes, I promise" and hugged Bhaskar.

A voice came from below the wedding altar, "Hey, hurry up, my wedding is also today." It was Sarika Di who lit our dramatic and emotional scene and finally, Bhaskar filled my maang and made me wear Mangalsutra and made me his forever.

Sarika di brought me to the room decorated for the wedding night and teased me by saying, "Take care of Bhaskar a little, do everything with ease, after all he is elder than you" and Sarika di started laughing.

"Di, he is experienced, you take care of Anand Jiju" I started laughing after saying this to Di and we both hugged each other.

After a while, Divyasha also came to the room with Bhaskar and from outside the room gave me a flying kiss and said "All the best, Niharika mummy" she winked at me and pushed Bhaskar inside and closed the room and went away and took Sarika di along with her.

"I am sorry, I know I would have made a big mistake by not accepting your love, but whatever it is, the truth between you and me is that I am older than you and I promise that I will try my best to ensure that you never realize this as long as I am alive.", Bhaskar said to me and came inside and sat next to me.

And finally that night came which had set my body on fire but how could I know what Bhaskar's mood was. But before I could say anything, Bhaskar took my hands in his hands and said "I want to make a confession"

"Yes, tell me," I said shyly

"I don't know whether I am right or wrong but still somewhere deep inside me there is a guilt and even today I feel that I was wrong and Ayesha was right, Maybe I'm a narcissist and she was right" Bhaskar had just started telling me but to stop him I put my lips on his lips and hugged him tightly and lay down on the bed with him.

The speed of our love was gradually increasing. I had just started kissing Bhaskar and to completely merge myself into his body, I slowly started removing his clothes. And when I dropped the wall of clothes and hugged Bhaskar's chest to mine, I truly felt his yearning and I was just feeling the softness of his hands while clinging to him. That feeling was very pure. Every touch of Bhaskar was purifying me. I could feel all the strings of my heart and mind getting connected to him and we became one, leaving behind all the sorrows and problems.

The folds of the sheet were clearly expressing the depth of our love. The night ended and with a new morning a new life began and when this morning dawned in Bhaskar's arms, my heart was dancing with joy but when Bhaskar got up from the bed, a question came to my mind and I asked "You had gone away, right? Then what happened that you came back, I want to know."

Bhaskar came and sat beside me and said, "Yes, I would have probably left. The train was standing at the station and I was just about to get on it when suddenly an old man held my hand and said" Bhaskar stopped saying this and got lost in some thought.

"What did he say" I asked

"A person who fails in love is sad, maybe very sad, but my child, those who lose in love can never get back up, they fall apart, they break down, Niharika loves you a lot and if you leave today, she will lose and I will not let her lose, go, she is waiting for you, the old man's words were piercing me like an arrow and I started feeling that by rejecting your love, I am insulting the one who gave me so much respect, I was going to defame her in front of the whole world and go away."

Bhaskar hugged me after saying this and then moved away with some fear and said, "I am sorry if I am being too cheap then I would like to apologize for that, it was just that I felt like hugging you."

"Now I am only yours Bhaskar, you can touch me whenever you want, you can hug me, why are you asking for forgiveness" I said

Bhaskar turned his back towards me and said "Maybe it has become a habit now, I always had to say sorry after touching her, so don't feel bad, I don't want to lose you, Niharika I love you very much"

I ran and took Bhaskar in my arms from behind and explained to him, "I too love you very much and not today, not now, not ever, I will never make you feel that you have done something wrong by touching me."

Our love was just blossoming when the door was knocked and Divyasha shouted from outside the gate "Niharika, mummy Bhaskar is yours now, you both stay locked in a room for as long as you wish but come now we all have to go to the temple"

"This girl, oh my god" I said and after saying "I love you" to Bhaskar and kissing his lips I quickly went to the bathroom

Bhaskar gave me a basket of flowers in the temple and went ahead with Divyasha to get sweets for Prasad.

I was moving forward with a basket of flowers remembering Mahadev, then a man collided with my hand and the basket of flowers fell from my hand. When I bent forward to pick up the basket, that man also started picking flowers with me and I was shocked to see him because he was none other than the one who had come to smoke cigarettes with me that day and had cleared my confusion.

He said, "I won't let you lose, my child, always be happy." Then, he smiled placed his hand on my head and got lost in the crowd of the temple.

And then in a loud voice the priest of the temple shouted "Har Har Mahadev, Shambhu"

Epilogue

Hey, where have you guys gone, this story is not over yet, today is our 20th wedding anniversary, and Bhaskar and Niharika, that is me, are very happy. Divyasha now lives in Mumbai and has become a chef in a famous hotel. She is also married to a doctor. By the way, her marriage is also a love marriage. Yes, it is not as strange as ours, but their life is going well.

Bhaskar got a job in the railways after that case, so he worked well for many years and also opened a health club in the park in front of our house. And now he has also given up smoking, although sometimes when we are in the mood, we both share the same cigarette and remember some old memories

Today, his pension comes and at least 700 people have joined Bhaskar's health club. I completed my studies here from Ajmer and decided to work here as a counseling psychologist. And yes, after three years of marriage, we had a daughter, whom we named Bani, Bhaskar and Niharika's Bani.

Well, you people may not want to know much about Ayesha's life, but since she was a part of this story, I will tell you. After that case, Ayesha was fired from her job and blacklisted, so she was forced to come to Ajmer and join her father's business and she ruined that business too because of her behavior. Today, no one wants to work in her father's business. She also fired the psychologist who was appointed for her because she still doesn't believe that she has made any mistake and she is a patient of narcissistic personality disorder.

You might remember that at the beginning of the story, I told you about a situation in which a man gets stuck in a room from where he cannot come out and we all assume that now nothing can be done to save him, but have we ever thought that even a single person can find a way from outside and take out the man stuck inside. All of us have our hopes connected to each other but nowadays man has trampled all hopes under his feet and by strangling his emotions he is just running behind the lie that he is the best and everyone else is below him.

Now, as far as I think, you must have understood why I told you that every person has a different thinking. In this story of my life, I have introduced you to people of every thinking, where on one hand Bhaskar, a man with clear thinking, sacrificed his life just for love, while on the other hand, his daughter Divyasha fought with her mother to save him and a girl who had nothing to do with all this, fell in love with a man who was much older than her.

And this way the pages of the book of my life kept filling up with happiness and Bhaskar and Niharika became one forever. Together we lived a life in which there was love and respect for each other's feelings.

See you......